Pucking Werewolves Book 2

My PUCKING Family

Izzy Elliott

Copyright © 2024 by Izzy Elliott

All rights reserved. No part of this publication may be reproduced, distributed, or transmitted in any form or by any means, including photocopying, recording, or other electronic or mechanical methods, without the prior written permission of the copyright owner, except in the use of brief quotations embodied in critical reviews.

ISBN 978-1-964220-06-2 (Paperback)
ISBN 978-1-964220-05-5 (Hardback)
ISBN 978-1-964220-04-8 (E-Book)

This is a work of fiction. Names, characters, places, and incidents either are the product of the author's imagination or are used fictitiously. Any resemblance to actual persons, living or dead events, or locales is entirely coincidental.

Edited by Jaquelyn Vale, She Who Edits LLC
Cover Designs by Izzy Elliott (cartoons by @ArtByToniii) and Aurelia Dunbar of Mayonaka Designs
Formatting by Aurelia Dunbar of Mayonaka Designs

Printed in the United States
Published by Izzy Elliott

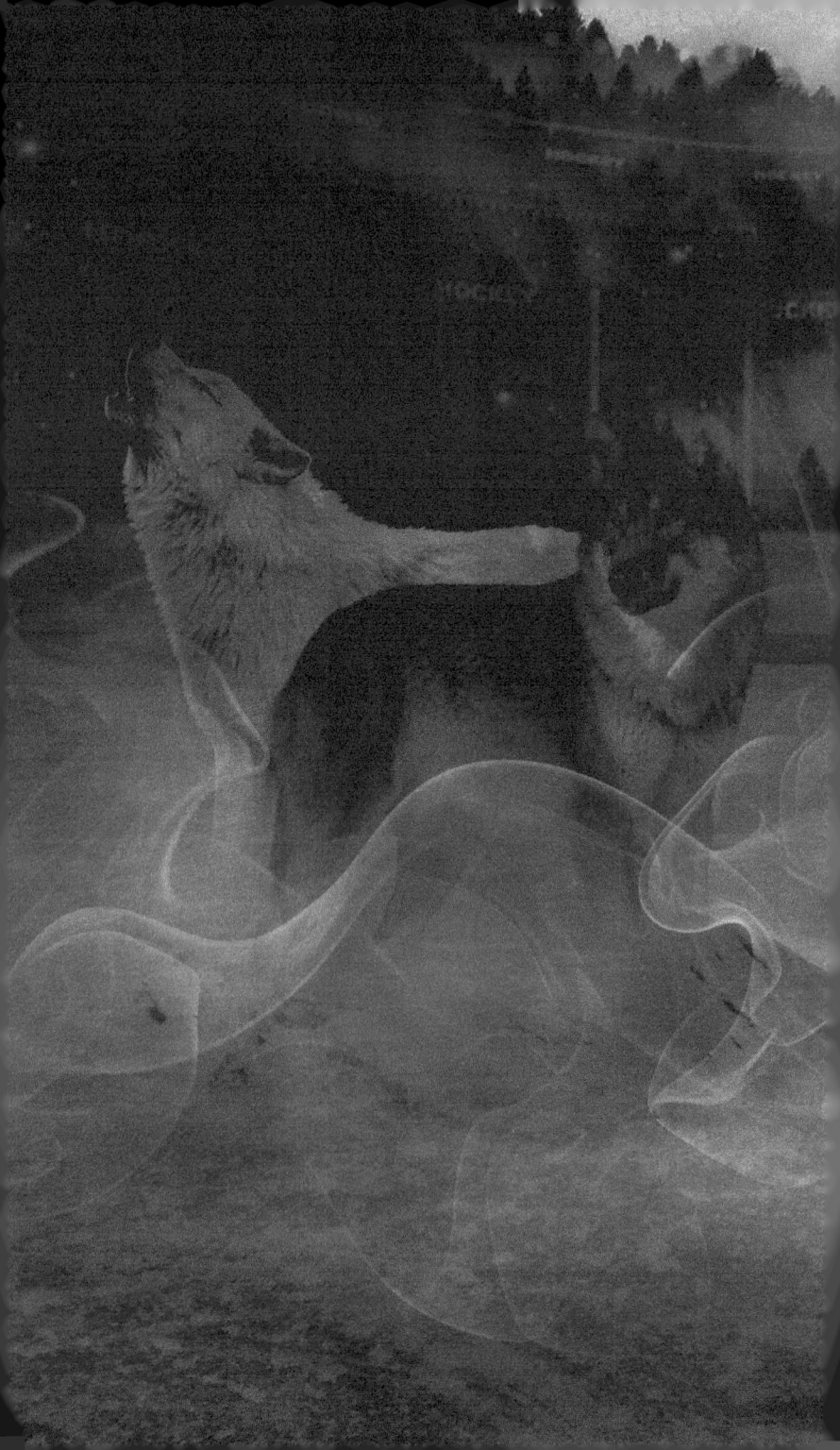

To every awkward and anxious girl who just wanted to live their idea of a "normal life" but keeps rolling with the punches and just doing the best she can. I see you.

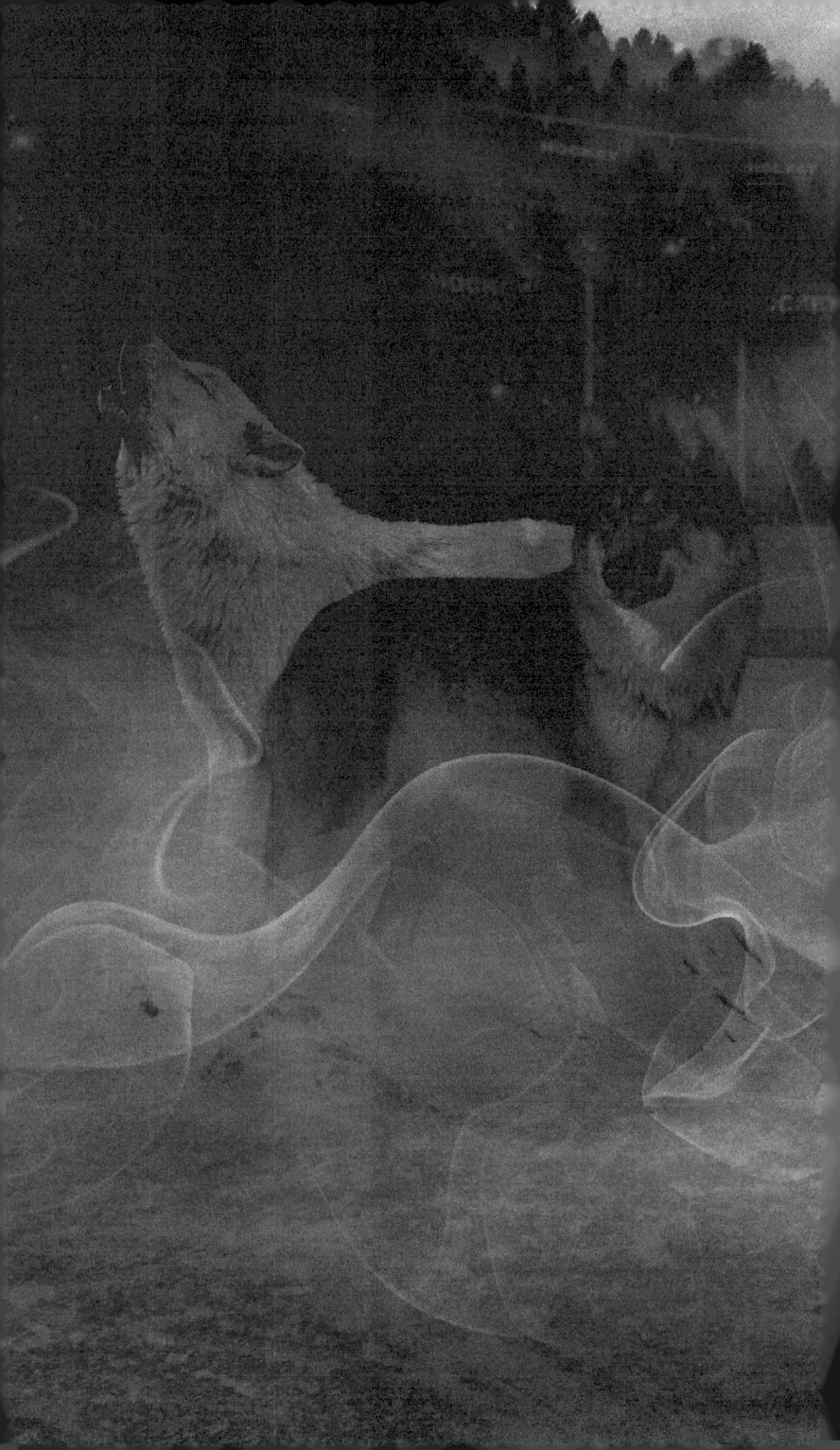

Note from the Author

Dear Reader,

My Pucking Family is a sweet, kind of insta-love romance story, but that doesn't mean there aren't darker moments. Please see below for a list of potential triggers. This book is also intended for adult readers (18+), as it contains explicit language and detailed sexual scenes.

If any of the following make you uncomfortable, please proceed with caution or consider choosing a different book.

The following may be triggering:

- Death of a parents, spouse, and child (flashbacks)
- Grief
- Anxiety
- Abduction
- Explicit language and scenes
- Unwanted Drug Use
- Death/Unaliving on page
- Blood

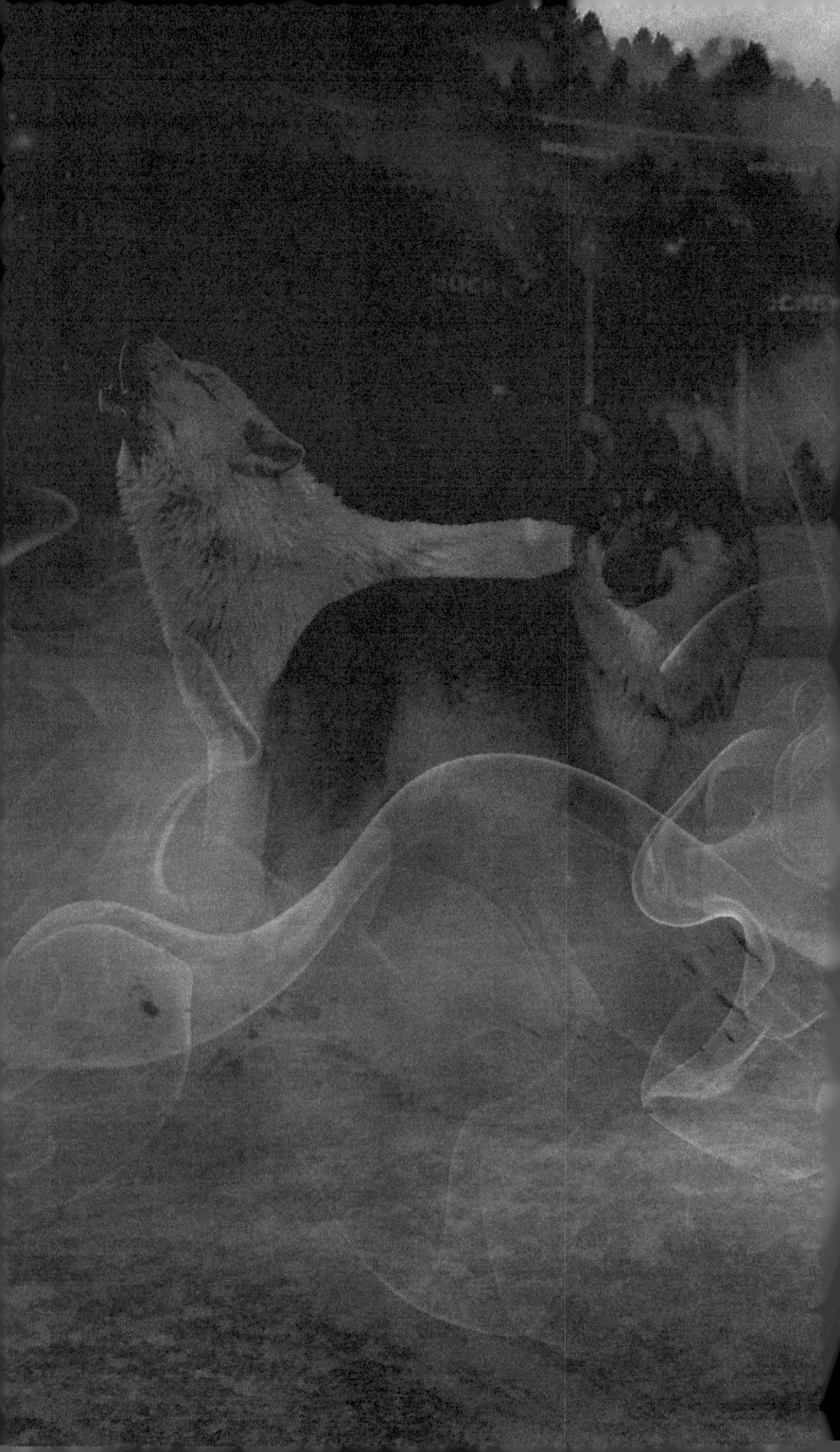

Before you continue!

My Pucking Family is the IMMEDIATE continuation of My Pucking Mate. This book begins in Roman's immediate next POV.

My Pucking Mate should be read first, as this is an on-going storyline and not interconnected standalones.

1
ROMAN

I'm still trying to wrap my head around how perfect last night was with Leera as I pull our car into the arena's parking lot.

It's strange to think that this is the same lot that fills to capacity on game nights—people cheering and hollering all over the place. During the day, it's calm, quiet, and desolate. The only cars parked here now are my teammates and a few abandoned cars, usually from responsible drivers who had too much to drink at the game last night and had to snag a ride home. I pull the car through to the other side of the aisle so that when I'm ready to leave, I can just drive out of the spot; not that it matters since the lot is practically deserted. It's mostly a reflex for game days.

I grab my bag and check my phone to see if Leera has texted me yet, but she hasn't. Being the impatient and slightly obsessed man that I am, I shoot her a text to let her know that I can't get her off my mind.

> Thank you for an amazing evening, my little miracle. When can I see you again?

But just as I hit send, I hear the chirp of her phone, here in the car somewhere. She must have dropped it in her scramble to get out of the car.

Benny, tell Coach I'll be late. I don't care what you tell him. Leera left her phone in my car, so I'm going to run it back to her.

Ten-four, Boss.

Tossing my gym bag back onto the floorboard, I scoop up the sparkly pink cell phone and keep it clutched in my left hand. I turn the car on, put it in gear, and take off back towards the college for one more moment with my sweet little mate.

This wasn't part of my plan to spend more time with her today, but I'm definitely not mad about it.

Her phone dings and rings a few times as I make the quick drive back to campus. It's Zoey's name that pops up continuously, and while I've crossed some boundaries, answering her phone or reading her texts with her best friend is crossing another kind of line, and I don't want to upset her. Her friend is probably wanting some girly gossip about last night anyway.

Bringing my thoughts back to last night sends sparks shooting through my blood stream. The way her body answered mine. The way it felt to sleep with her in my arms. Knowing I have to take my time with her makes every moment that much sweeter. Knowing as I claim her body, in every way it can be claimed, that I will be the first and only person to bring her body pleasure, is enough to make my dick hard just at the thought, and I have to set her phone down long enough to adjust myself.

Like the arena, the college grounds are strangely quiet on the weekends. Most kids elect not to have weekend classes, and they usually find better things to do with their time than hang out and do nothing on campus. For so many, like Leera, it's their first taste of freedom, so they're sure to fill their time with adventures, some more appropriate than others. But still, this emptiness…I can't explain it. Something feels wrong, but I can't pinpoint what it is.

When I pull up in front of her dorm building, I'm immediately on even higher alert when I find her roommate running across the lot towards me. *Fuck what was her name…Chloe or something. No, it started with a Z…zzz…Zoey; it's Zoey.* As she nears me, she's not just running, she's panicking. Her face is red, and her eyes are wild. I scramble out of the car and sprint the remaining distance between us.

"Zoey, what's wrong?" I ask the poor girl who looks like she's on the verge of hyperventilating.

For too many moments, she just shakes her head and sobs.

My wolf and I are both about to lose our shit at this point.

Placing my hands firmly on her shoulders, I attempt to ground her all while trying not to scare her at the same time, and I try again, "Zoey," I growl, "Can you hear me? What's going on? Is Leera okay? Where is she?" My own panic is now setting in as I try to understand what we're even upset about. I take a moment to look around her, but I don't see Leera anywhere. Surely, it's nothing. Maybe they just got into an argument or something.

She takes a few more long breaths, trying to regain what she wasn't able to get in before. She seems to be getting herself together enough to speak, while I'm starting to tingle with a deadly combination of terror and rage. I don't like this feeling. I need information. I need this small human to pull her shit together and tell me what the fuck is going on.

"She's gone! I can't find her anywhere! I went back to the room, and I could see she was back because some of her stuff was there. Not all her stuff; her school stuff was missing. So I came back out to see if maybe we just missed each other. I told her to come out and study with me under our tree. But when I came back out, all I found was her backpack on the ground." She finally stops dumping all her thoughts on me at once and grabs my hand, dragging me across the grass while I try to keep my mind and body here and now. I can feel my wolf trying to take control, but I have to fight it.

Just outside the door to their dorm building, there are wolf scents I don't recognize swallowing the sweet honeysuckle and spun sugar smell of my girl. But they're faint. There's some grass ripped out of the ground and scuffs in the dirt, like someone was dragging their feet. A few more steps from that area is her backpack. Not just sitting on the ground like she stepped away to grab something real quick. It's laying on its top, like it'd been thrown down in a hurry.

From there, to the very edge of the parking lot, closest to the grass, are more scuffle marks. These look more erratic. I'm not the tracker. Benny is. But I know well enough to recognize a kidnapping.

My entire body is shaking, and I don't know if it's from the rage consuming my entire being or the fear threatening to drown me alive.

BENNNNNNYYYYY! I scream through the mind link just as my wolf begins to howl. I can feel my soul starting to shred.

I can't go through this again. Why is history repeating itself?

It wasn't even humans who took her. It was wolves. Wolves who I don't know. Who would even know about her other than the six of us?

That's when I remember the stunt I pulled at the game. Making a grand gesture of love to my soul mate. "GODDAMMIT!" I roar out loud this time, causing Zoey to jump nearly a foot off the ground. In the midst of my nightmare coming true, I forgot she was even here.

Shit Boss, what's up? All the men heard you…
We're listening…
What's going on?
Are you okay?!
My men all shout through our bond.

"Zoey, can you sit down right here while I try to figure out what happened here?" I ask her as gently as I can, though it must not have actually been gentle judging by the way her body tenses, but she just nods and sniffles.

She's gone. They have her. I don't know who they are… Benny, I can't do this again. I'm half roaring, half wailing for all my men to hear, but I can't be bothered to care right now.

I'm breaking. This is all too much. It's all my fault. For many moments, there is no response, but I can feel their energies. They're all furious and terrified. Not just for me but for her. For such a small creature, she truly evokes large feelings in everyone she meets. It rips me apart even more to know how much they already care for her as well.

FUCK…
GODDAMMIT…
SHIT…
My men all take turns venting their frustration through their

chosen words, while they also try to wrap their heads around what's happening.

I'll tell Coach what's going on, and he'll understand why we've got to leave practice. Benny leads, having been the first one to gather himself, apparently. That's one of the perks of the sport being primarily werewolf blood; they understand pack and mate matters that would otherwise be a disaster to try and dance around when shit like this happens. Only most people don't have to deal with shit like this. With their mate being kidnapped.

I'll set up a trace on her—

I have to interrupt Slate mid-sentence. *I have her phone. She dropped it in my car. I was bringing it back to her. That's how I found out she was missing.*

My wolf continues to howl in rage as I grow anxious, fearful of what's to come because…I don't think we can survive this a second time.

FUCK is Slate's only response. The man is our technology contact for a reason. He can trace and hack pretty much anything. I don't know what he can do without anything to track.

We're on our way, Boss. We'll find her. I promise.

I know Benny's just trying to make me feel better, but the way he sounds right now, it's not working. That man radiates sunshine and happiness, and even he sounds dark and concerned.

I can't do this again. If something happens to her, I'll…

I'm snapped out of my own thoughts when I hear a fresh sob come from Zoey.

"Roman, where is she?!" she yells at me like it's all my fault. It probably is.

Why did I allow myself to think that this time would be any different?

She jumps from where she's sitting and bangs her fists on my chest for a few moments. She's in worse shape than I initially noticed, and my anger must be suffocating her.

"I don't, FUCK, I don't know. I just came back to drop off her cellphone. She dropped it in the car." I grab hold of Zoey's still swinging fists, and as calmly as I can, I capture her hands to end her ineffective assault. She stares at me for a minute and steps away, wrapping her arms around her middle.

Without being able to do anything until my men get here, I pace the grass in front of Zoey with my head in my hands.

Anger and unease go to war within me as I do everything in my power to resist the urge to transform into a wolf because a human is in my presence. It would be so much easier to release control to my wolf and allow the darkness and foreboding to consume me.

"Did you see her at all or have any idea who took her? Has she been…has she been talking to anyone else?" I ask, not really wanting to know the answer.

"Are you fucking stupid or something?! She's crazy about you, you giant idiot! I called the police forever ago; where are they?!" she yells, on the verge of another meltdown. Just as she throws herself down to the grass, we hear the sirens approaching in the distance.

2
Leera

Ugh, I feel like total crap, I think as I try to wake up from my nightmare.

That was so weird.

Wait, why does my whole body hurt?

Why does it feel like I'm lying on cold concrete?

Why can't I…

…My thoughts even feel fuzzy…

…What's going on?

I can't open my eyes.

I continue to struggle to force my body to listen to my brain, but nothing's happening.

OH MY GOD! It wasn't a dream.

It all comes back to me.

The amazing night with Roman.

Him bringing me home.

Going outside to study with Zoey…

…being kidnapped…

I can't even cry because my body won't respond.

Maybe if I try to… my thoughts are cut off by another sharp pain in what I think is my neck before I fall back into the dark depths of the nothingness.

3
ROMAN

I've always wondered why there aren't more supernatural beings on the police force. These mere mortal men are so far out of their league, and they don't even know it. What's worse is that mortal laws and regulations are so fucked that there's nothing they can do because she has only been missing for an hour or so.

Apparently a college student won't even be considered a missing person unless it's been more than twenty-four hours. It doesn't matter that her bag and phone are here without her. It doesn't matter that there's absolutely no sign of her. Because no one saw her be abducted, she may not "actually" be missing.

Fucking idiots.

As much as I want to beat the two officers to a pulp, I know it's not their fault the system is flawed. I just try to keep my shit together until they're gone.

Once they finally take their leave, they hand me and Zoey their worthless contact information.

Zoey is still yelling at them, and I barely stop her when she picks up a rock and pulls her arm back to throw it in their direction.

This little human is a fireball, and she loves my Leera. Their friendship runs deep, and that means there will probably be a lot of her in my life moving forward. That is, assuming I can find my mate and my life isn't over. Right now, I need her to calm down and go inside so my men and I can figure out a game plan.

Convincing Zoey to go inside isn't easy either, and I'm quickly losing the battle with my restraint. Slate comes over—his cool and collected self—and convinces her that the best way she can help would be to stay in her dorm in case Leera shows up. He even walks her inside to make sure she listens.

I will burn this realm to the ground to find her if I have to. I know she's alive because, even though we haven't completed the mate bond, I would still know if something happened to her.

With the way our bonds work, you can feel very strong emotions in a closer space, but even someone who never met their mate would know if they died. The snapping of that living link would be excruciating. They'd be able to survive it, but living an immortal existence and knowing you can never find the other half of your soul is a miserable thought.

I can't think straight. The terror of my reality is too heavy, and it's slowly crushing me. My men aren't in much better spirits, and all of our wolves are ready to go to war.

As soon as Benny got here, he was in full tracker mode and tried to gather any additional information but came up short. There are a lot of really impactful technological advancements in this current world, but it also makes things like tracking people harder. So many vehicles are so secure that scents don't filter out of them. So once they shut the doors, the trail goes cold.

Since this godforsaken college doesn't have security cameras on the parking lots, we have no idea what vehicle she's in or where they're headed.

Why did she have to drop her fucking phone in the car this morning?

Was it my fault?

Was it the kiss goodbye?

Who took her?

Why did they take her?

I feel my men approach, but I already know what they're going to say. There's nothing we can do right now, and we need to go home and do what we can from there.

Slate is going to run her photo through facial recognition and screen all the traffic cameras in the area. If they have her in a car with regular windows, we might get lucky.

Eris and Dolos are going to use their spy skills from the army back home to track down our enemies and see if they can find anything out. It's naive to think that an ancient foe or rival wouldn't be involved.

Andrei looks as green as I feel. Seriously, is he going to throw up? *Andrei, you good brother?* He just shakes his head and walks away.

Well, okay then.

I walk inside to talk to Zoey before we leave. I knock on the door and wait as I hear her shuffling around the room.

She barely cracks open the door, and her eyes are red and puffy. "The guys and I are going to head out. Here's my number. Please let me know if you hear anything. Go ahead and text me so that I have your number, and I'll do the same."

She accepts my phone number, but she doesn't look at me.

She just nods her head a little and slowly shuts the door in my face. A moment later, my phone pings with the requested text, and I program her number into my phone.

I need to get out of here.

I need to go for a run.

I need to find my mate.

I burst through the door of the building, leaving my car on the lot for now. I have to shift. I need to let go and give myself to my wolf for a while. I've run all the way across campus when I finally hit an area wooded enough that I can let myself go.

I step behind the overgrown brush and stash my clothes for when I'm finished. Thick cream-colored fur replaces my smooth golden skin as a deep, mournful howl is ripped from my body. My wolf is livid. He's blaming me for dropping her off this morning because he just doesn't get it. It's not like it was five or six hundred years ago. Hell, I don't even know how old my soul truly is. And no matter how much we want to, we can't just claim our women and keep them with us for every moment.

I run until it feels like my legs might actually fall off, and it still doesn't feel long enough. How the fuck am I supposed to do anything until we find her. We have an away game in two days and are supposed to fly out tomorrow morning. How the fuck am I supposed to give a fuck about hockey when she's all I can think about?

I've circled back to campus so I can grab my clothes and car I left here so many hours ago. I hate the sight of the campus and all these people carrying on with their lives like my whole world isn't crumbling. Like my reason for living isn't missing. Not missing. Taken.

I throw myself into the car and hope the guys have something—anything—when I get home.

4
Leera

Come on, Leera, you can do this.
Pull harder.
Pull yourself out of this darkness.
I will not die here.

I'm trying so hard to bring myself out of this horrible unconsciousness. The first time, it was all darkness. This time, I kept reliving the best and worst moments of my life.

Who took me?
Why was I taken?
Will I ever see Roman again?

I still can't open my eyes, but I'm shooting off brain signals to every inch of my body, hoping and praying that something will move. Anything.

How long have I been here?
Is anyone looking for me?

Just when I feel like giving up, I feel my foot twitch. It was the tiniest twitch, but it's the only physical reaction I've gotten from my body in…well, since I was thrown into that van.

Focus Leera.
Do it again.

I'm able to recreate the twitch in my foot. I focus all my energy on that one limb. If I can start there, maybe I can work my way up my body and bring my motion back.

All of a sudden, my leg doesn't just twitch, it flies forward, connecting hard with something, causing a sharp pain to shoot through my shin. I can't open my eyes to see what I hit. I can't even cry out.

That's when I notice the sound of shuffled footsteps approaching me. My leg kicking…whatever I kicked…must have alerted my captors.

Please go away! Leave me alone.

I want to scream and fight, but my body just can't.

What kind of drug did they give me?
How do I fight this?

My leg twitches one more time before I again feel the now familiar prick of a needle in my neck as the world fades away, and this time, I don't fight the darkness.

5
ROMAN

As I pull my car into the garage level of our building, I approach my parking spot, and I'm immediately ready to murder someone again. Preferably the person standing in front of my spot. She's standing there with her hands on her hips, like I've inconvenienced her by making her wait for something.

I throw the car into park and barrel out of my seat, slamming the door for good measure.

"What the fuck are you doing here, India?!" I roar, but she doesn't even flinch. She's just staring at me. It's not sweet, but it's not evil either. She's strangely impassive.

"I came to watch your game. I'm trying to be more active and supportive. And what do I find, Roman? You making heart eyes at some human bitch?" It takes every ounce of willpower I possess not to lay her out, but she's not done yet, and her voice changes to something I don't know that I've ever heard. She sounds almost…real.

"Look, I know I've never been your favorite person. I know

I haven't lived my life in the best light. I know you'll never love me, but the King chose us. He chose us to lead our people. I'm taking that responsibility seriously. I'm trying to change. But walking in and seeing that last night…"

Is this really happening to me?!

"…I'm sorry for my attitude, okay. Just give me a chance for us to try to do this right."

I can't even think right now. While I no longer want to lay her out, I also can't tell her right now that there isn't, and never will be, an us. I want to scream it from the rooftops that I don't care about the crown and the responsibility to our people. I don't care about any of it. I need to find my fucking mate, and that's it for me. She's it for me.

"India, I appreciate the sentiment. I really do, and I'm proud of you for trying to change. But I really can't talk about this right now," I growl. "Something has come up, and I have to get upstairs to the men. I'll call you when I'm ready to talk, okay?"

I swear, a small look of triumph crosses her features for a fleeting moment, but I chalk it up to me not raging at her and throwing her out on her ass. She thinks I took the bait. I'm also proud of myself for my response. She has no idea what's going on.

She nods and touches my arm. I want to flinch. My wolf is snarling at her. But I force myself to remain completely still. "I'm here for you, Roman. Let me know when you're ready to talk, and I'll be here." She definitely thinks she won. She pats my arm and turns on her heels, swaying her hips as she walks away, obviously hoping I'm watching her for reasons other than making sure she leaves. Just as she reaches her car, she opens the door, turns, and gives me a small smile and wave before setting herself into the seat and closing the door.

As soon as she's out of sight, I sprint to the elevator door and catch the men up on the encounter through our mind link as I ride up to the main level.

I burst through the door and find them all waiting by the massive kitchen island, right where I'd hoped they'd be.

"Alright, report. Do we have anything?" I ask, already knowing the answer. If they had anything, they would have already told me through our mind link. I didn't block them out, so I would have heard anything.

The only answers I get are shaking heads and somber faces.

"FUCK!" I roar, slamming the door so hard it splinters.

I tear into the kitchen and start destroying anything that I can reach. Ripping glass plates out of the cabinets to crash them to the ground. Just to feel something. Anything. Blind rage will have to do for now. My men let me continue my rampage through half of the kitchen before I'm being sprayed with cold water.

Still lost in the fury, I turn around with every intention of murdering whoever is responsible.

Instead, I'm now being sprayed in the face with a steady stream of ice cold water. It's hitting me square between the eyes, so I can't even see who I want to kill.

I take two steps towards the source of the spray when it stops. My anger slowly dissipates as I find Matilda standing beside the sink, placing the nozzle back onto the kitchen faucet. She sets her hands on her hips and steps towards me slowly.

"Come here, dear," she commands in her no-nonsense voice, but I'm frozen in place, other than shaking my head.

"Tsk, tsk, tsk. What a mess you've made." She shakes her

head as she scans the area. Likely thinking of how long it will take her to clean this up. She's also probably taking a mental inventory of everything I destroyed so she can replace it.

Shame seeps into my bones at my outburst as I lower my head and begin picking things up, when a small wrinkled hand crosses my line of vision and takes my hand in hers.

"Roman, dear, look at me," she tries again.

I slowly lift my head, afraid that she can see straight into my soul and see how worthless I really am.

"The boys caught me up on what's going on," she continues as she slowly tugs me towards a barstool beside Benny. "Losing your cool won't help that poor girl or yourself. Get your shit together, young man."

"Miss Tilly!" Benny shrieks in shocked laughter. "You never say bad words."

"Well, maybe you boys are finally rubbing off on me. Either way, you boys need to find our girl."

I've never been so motivated by such few words, but I let them soak into my skin as I look around the room, and it seems to have hit all my men the same way.

"You're right. I'm sorry for the mess. I'll clean it up, and you can use my card to replace everything with whatever you like." Turning towards my men, I ask, "What are we going to do about the away game coming up?" I ask no one in particular.

Slate is the first to respond, "Well, I have a plan to have the game cancelled with your approval."

My only response is the lift of my eyebrow and nod for him to continue.

He begins typing on his ever-present laptop before turning it to me. "I checked their system to be sure I could pull it off before I offered, but if I hack the other team's rink systems, I can shut down the coolant system and melt the ice, so they'll have no choice but to reschedule the game."

"Do it," I answer without a second thought. "I'm in no headspace to play a game. If you all want to go play without me, you're more than wel—"

"Not fucking happening, Boss," Benny pipes up immediately. "Where you go, we go."

The twins cross their arms over their chests and nod.

Andrei, the poor kid, looks as fucked up about all this as I feel.

"Alright, Eris, Dolos, do you have anything on our least favorite people?"

"Nah, most of them don't even hold a grudge anymore," Eris speaks first, sounding disappointed that more people weren't out to get us.

"Thanks to Slate's hacking skills, I was able to check on Khaos, and it looks like he is throwing a charity event for his team tonight," Dolos provides.

I look to Andrei again, but he just shakes his head and walks away again.

Slate's head is still buried in his laptop when I ask, "What can I do?" I loathe how desperate I sound.

"Give me some time. I'll find something. I swear."

With that, I leave the room and climb the steps to the roof.

6
Leera

I learned my lesson last time I started to capture my consciousness. Don't start with limbs that can give me away. This time, I'm starting with my face. I need to get my eyes to open. I need to see where I am. I need to see who has taken me. I need to see ANYTHING so I can try to find a way out of here.

Of course it can't be as simple as willing my eyelids to open and cooperate just because I want them to. I will never take the simple neurological reactions of my body for granted ever again.

Since my eyelids are still on hiatus, I focus on my eyeballs. With my eyes closed, I pour all of my will into simply moving my eyes back and forth beneath the lids.

I don't know how much time has passed, but I will not die here. Wherever the hell here is.

Wait, was that a twitch? I honestly can't tell if my eye really moved or if I imagined it.

The thought barely has time to be absorbed as I feel it again.

I'm making progress. I can do this.

While I continue to focus on moving my eyeballs, I hear

heavy steps. They sound as though they are descending, so either I'm in some kind of basement, or it's a two-story house and they are upstairs. I need to gather all the information I can about my surroundings. No matter how small.

The steps continue towards me before stopping. I'm drowning in the silence when another set of steps, less heavy than the first, walk the same path as the first person, but everything else is still silent.

I steady my breathing as best as I can to try and hide my growing panic. I don't want them to drug me again. Last time they did, it was my own fault for giving myself away.

It feels like an eternity passes before they begin speaking in hushed tones, so low I have to use all my focus to hone in on the sounds of their voices. I don't recognize either one of them, not that I know that many people to compare them to. One sounds like some rich, bossy dude, and the other sounds like maybe he's just the hired help.

"Has she moved again?" Bossy Rich Dude asks.

"Not yet," Hired Help answers, sounding irritated.

"We need to find a way to dispose of her once the dust settles. I need her out of my way."

How the hell am I in this dude's way when I don't even recognize his voice? I know less than ten people, and I've managed to upset someone enough to need to be DISPOSED of?!

Calm down, Leera. Panic will only let them know you're awake. Breathe steadily. Think of happy things. Pink fuzzy blankets. Cool Beans coffee. Roman.

The last one threatens to rip a small sob from my body at the possibility of never seeing him again. At the thought of him going through the pain of losing a second mate.

He won't lose another mate because you're going to survive this. Whatever this is. Now keep breathing as normally as possible, keep trying to move your eyes, and listen.

I lost myself to my thoughts for so long I don't know how much of their conversation I missed. Bossy Rich Dude is still talking, "They're definitely aware of her absence, and it's causing quite the spectacle."

"Why's everyone making such a big deal over some little orphaned college chick?" Hired Help asks.

"She's so much more than that. None of the details are your concern. Do what you're paid to do and nothing else," Bossy Rich Dude huffs out. I can hear one of them leave the room.

Steps approach me slowly, and I freeze, trying not to let them see my attempt at moving my eyeballs so that I can hopefully appear to remain unconscious.

After several moments, the unknown man seems to be convinced, and I hear him also leave the space and ascend to wherever else there is to go.

I wait a few extra minutes to make sure that I'm truly alone before I return to the task at hand. Knowing I'm alone, I give my eyelids the mental signal to open, and to my surprise, they very slowly respond to my plea.

While everything is extremely blurry, MY EYES ARE OPEN! I rapidly blink my eyes, trying to clear away the drug-induced haze. A bajillion blinks later, the area is coming into focus.

Definitely a basement. I'm lying on an old, worn, army green sleeping bag along the far wall. There is a large concrete floor beneath me and a couple of wooden beams connecting the floor to the wooden rafters above. I wouldn't really call it a ceiling since the space is clearly unfinished. There are two swinging, single lightbulbs in place to illuminate the space, but only the one farthest from me is on. The one closest to me is either burned out or turned off, leaving my body lying in the darkest part of the room. The stairs are the farthest point from my body and are also bare wood.

Having taken in and catalogued my surroundings, I bring myself back to waking each part of my body. Since my eyes cooperated first, I try to turn my head. I don't get a reaction immediately, so I just keep begging my brain, *just turn half way around,* and my body answers my call! Now that my head is cooperating, I lift it up to check my body for any signs of assault. Tears sting my eyes when I find myself completely intact.

Okay, okay, I can do this!

Next step, my arms, but I'll start with my fingers. The next several minutes are spent focusing all my power on moving my fingers. Just a little wiggle to let me know that I'm making progress. The panic begins to swell again. *Why can't my anxiety remain paralyzed?* I focus on my grounding tools. Taking my attention away from moving my fingers to calm my terrified heart. *I don't have time to be scared if I want to get out of this.*

After taking a handful of deep breaths and naming an animal for each letter of the alphabet, moving backwards from Z to A, I've calmed myself down enough to stave off the panic attack that so badly wants to consume my body.

To my surprise, my fingers wiggle without as much work this time, and I thank whatever gods above for the small reprieve.

Okay, fingers wiggling, check. Now my arms. Alright, *body, let's do this.* I start with a simple twirl of my wrist, and again, it answers immediately. It's slow, but it's still moving. I continue to roll it in a clockwise motion a few times. Then do the same with the other hand. I see a sudden small flash of light, and my heart begins stampeding in my chest at the thought of being caught moving.

I instantly still myself, bracing for the worst, but nothing comes. No one is here. *What was that light?* I look around the space again and confirm there aren't windows, so it's not like a car drove by with lights on or something.

Is it even daylight outside or the middle of the night? As a reflex, I lift my arm to check the time on my smartwatch. *MY SMARTWATCH! That's what the light was! IT'S NOT DEAD! OH MY GOD. And my body responded to the reflex without forceful thought.* A small whimper does escape me as I fight to hold in the ugly cries trying to wreck my body.

Focus Leera. The battery is almost dead. As quickly as my fingers can move in their groggy state, I type up a text to Roman. Just as I hit send, my watch powers down, and I don't know if it sent my message before it shut down.

At that, I allow a few tears to escape.

I spend a few more minutes moving different parts of my body to find I've regained most of my control.

Using all this time and strength to regain function of myself has drained my body's battery, and I find myself falling back into the darkness. At least this time it's my choice, and not from a needle.

No sooner than the thought passes do I hear the descent of heavy footsteps again. I try to drag myself back to the light to beg them to leave me alone, but I used every ounce of stamina I had. "Sorry, Doll Face, can't have you waking up and ruining things," Hired Help says as I feel the stick of yet another needle in my neck.

My Pucking Family

I'm so sorry, Roman. I tried.

7
ROMAN

I thought coming up here and sitting under the simple twinkle lights she loved so much would help, but it's only causing the ache to intensify.

I considered tearing this all apart. Shredding it all to scraps of nothing, but that won't help either. And she loved it. She'll expect it to be here when she gets home. Because she's coming home. She has to.

Sitting in the same place we sat the night I decorated it all for her, I allow my head to fall back against the cushions and let it all wash over me. The rage, the terror, the uselessness, the pain, the failure. This is all my fault. My wolf huffs in agreement. *I deserve that.*

I've been sitting here for hours, wallowing in my fear, allowing it to swallow me whole. The sun is starting to set, and it's dragging my hope below the horizon with it.

I force myself to my feet with the intention of going back inside to clean up the mess I made in the kitchen. I'll be even more pissed at myself if, because I fucked that off all day, Matilda ended up cleaning up after me. My phone pings with what I hope is an update from one of my men, but they don't really text me.

One look at the screen has me flying through the rooftop door and down the stairs to where Slate is still sitting in the exact same spot. The only change is the cord attached to his laptop to prevent its death and an additional laptop beside it.

"Leera just texted me from her number. I don't know how that's possible when we have her phone, though!" I'm yelling as I approach him. At the sound of my voice, Benny races into the kitchen area as well, with the twins hot on his heels.

Slate snatches the phone from my hands and starts typing like a madman on one of his laptops, with all of us hanging over his shoulder, like we'd understand anything on the screen anyway.

He shakes his head as he mumbles to himself, "I'm so fucking stupid. I should have thought about that. Goddammit, Boss, I should have thought about that. I'm so fucking sorry."

"Should have thought about what?! WHERE IS SHE?!" I roar, my chest rising and adrenaline pumping through me as I impatiently wait for an answer. "Doesn't she wear one of those smartwatches?" he asks as the realization dawns on all of us. We could have tracked her this whole time.

"Yes, she's always using it for alarms and appointments and reminders. I didn't know those could be tracked."

"Some of them can't, but the ones like hers that are connected to the networks can be. I'm not able to pull a signal from it now, but I can triangulate the general area from the towers her text pinged off of," he says as he continues to type furiously on both laptop keyboards.

In only a few minutes, he locates a one-mile area for us to

search. We crash around, grabbing our things on our way out of the townhouse to get our girl, as Matilda calls her. Fuck! I didn't clean the kitchen. I'm going to owe that little woman big time. But that can wait until we get my mate back.

We reach the garage, and my men turn to me for instruction.

"We take two cars in case shit hits the fan."

They instinctively split into two groups. One group takes Benny's lifted, white truck, and the other group takes the black SUV with dark tinted windows.

Benny and the twins in his. Slate, Andrei, and I in the SUV.

I am hoping that driving will help channel some of the burning, electric intensity surging through my body, but nothing will help until she is safe in my arms.

According to the GPS directions Slate loaded to the SUV's navigation system, she's only been twenty fucking minutes away this entire gods-damn time!

I've never been so pissed and happy about something at the same time in my entire existence.

We approach a new neighborhood development area. There are what looks to be about fifty mid-construction homes scattered throughout the new subdivision. We initially drive by to ensure the area isn't crawling with whoever—or whatever—took Leera from me.

Seeing no signs of life in the extended area, we park on the outskirts of the neighborhood's boundaries in the black of night.

She's in this neighborhood somewhere. I can't get a solid direction on her location because her scent is so faint on the light breeze.

I take off my clothes and throw them in the back of Benny's

truck without a second thought, my men following my lead.

We're surrounded with the sounds of bones crunching and snarls as we give our wolves control of our bodies.

Benny's wolf is ready first. He's all cinnamon-red fur and muscles, as he nods to me with a snarl.

The twins' wolves are next, in their matching forms. They're both leaner than Benny and I, but it works to help them slink about when needed. They're both solid gray with the exception of their tails; that's the only way you can tell them apart in wolf form. Eris has a black tip on the end of his tail, while the tip of Dolos' tail is white.

Andrei comes snarling up to the group in his large brindled wolf form, as Slate casually approaches still in human form, checking his laptop one last time before exploding into a solid onyx-black wolf, pawing at the ground.

In an instant, we're sprinting through the development, trusting my wolf to lead us to our mate. Her scent is slowly getting stronger, but so is that of the other unknown wolves.

When I'm certain we're about to approach the house where they must be keeping her, I hear the skip of a rock on the pavement to my right. *Hold it, men; we've got company.* With my men to my left, I whip my body to the right and capture the man, who is still in human form, by the throat and rip it out, hopefully preventing him from alerting anyone of our arrival. Benny's huff in approval is all it takes for us to continue our pursuit.

Judging by the scents in the air, we have one or two more men to take care of before we can safely get Leera out of here. Swinging my head in either direction, I send my men to circle the house and take care of any others as I approach the nearly finished home in front of me.

I shift back into my human form to comfortably fit inside the house and survey my surroundings as Eris calls out through our mind link, *Got one,* while Dolos bitches that he wanted him.

The house is massive. Open concept like our townhouse, but it hasn't been painted yet. The drywall on the walls is still covered in spots from the builders using mud to cover the screws and divots. There is a pile of cabinets sitting in what I assume will be the kitchen, waiting to be installed. Just on the other side of the kitchen area is an empty chair next to a door, where the last guard must have been sitting.

I think she's being kept in the basement. I'm going down.
Heard.

I slowly turn the knob on the door, and it doesn't creak or squeak, and I'm thankful for the new building. There's a light on at the bottom of the stairs, and in that moment, I know she's here. But so is someone else. No longer caring for discretion, I throw my body down the stairs as fast as my legs can go.

The greasy slime ball of a man rounds the stairs just as I reach the bottom. My wolf wants to rip his head from his body, but we need answers, so I settle for kicking his right knee backwards, listening for the sound of the bones snapping as he wails. The bones will heal fast, so I kick him in the chest, knocking the wind from his body as Benny catches up to us. He grabs the man from behind and holds onto him as the twins approach, ready to carry him out of here. He's thrashing and growling and likely about to shift, so Slate punches him right behind the ear and knocks him out to save us the trouble.

It only takes a second to find her; she's laying on her back at the far side of the basement in the dark. She's barely breathing. Checking for her pulse, she doesn't even stir. Her pulse is incredibly low as well. They must have been keeping her drugged.

I kneel and lay my body over hers and take a moment to treasure the feel of her living body under mine. The moment is reminiscent of finding Imogen, but I made it this time. I made it to *her* in time.

We don't have time for me to give in to my emotions, so I hold them back as I scoop her tiny body into my arms. I stand and turn to find Andrei waiting for me. His eyes glaze over when he sees her limp body in my arms as we climb the stairs.

As soon as the twins give the all clear, we sprint out of this house and away from the neighborhood.

Slate's waiting in the driver's seat of the SUV, the truck already having left with the twins, Benny, and the man we found. I climb into the back seat with her in my lap as Andrei throws me my clothes before slamming the door and catapulting himself into the passenger seat. Slate peels out onto the road to take us home. I set Leera on the seat next to me only long enough to slide my pants on before I'm scooping her back up and plastering our bodies together, whispering everything I wanted to say to her that I held back. Whispering everything I wish I could have said to Imogen had I found her in time. Promising that this will never happen again. Promising her the world.

8
Leera

*Mhmmm...*I'm warm as my consciousness tries to remind me something is wrong, but I can't be bothered to care. My body is warm and content. There's a purring sound rumbling within me, matched by a deeper purring rumble underneath my face, and I'm smothered with the intoxicating scent of cherries and leather.

*Wait...that's not right...*I remind myself that I should be terrified, but I can't seem to remember why...*why can't I remember wha...*

My thoughts trail off as my eyes fly open, and I throw my body into the seated position, causing me to sway with light-headedness. The late morning light streaming through the curtains blinds me for a moment.

The room immediately erupts into complete disarray at my unexpected movement, and I find myself panting and trying to avoid passing out from hyperventilating as it all comes flooding back to me.

I was kidnapped...and drugged.

I was lying on a cold, concrete floor, trying to find a way out. Needed to find a way back to...

"Roman," I sob as I fling myself into his unexpecting form. His hands, previously scrubbing his scalp with worry, immediately capture my body without hesitance.

I'm pretty sure we're both crying now as I cling to him. I was scared for me, but my soul was tortured for what Roman was going through in my absence.

Our bodies fit together like pieces of a puzzle as he holds me. Each dip and curve of his body is filled with mine. No amount of air or light could come between us right now.

As I finally lift my head from his chest, I pull myself to my knees in front of him and take his face in my hands. My hands look so small against this man, even smaller when he raises his to softly cover mine, and they seem to vanish.

I'm still crying. I can't speak. I don't know how long we've been sitting here trying to grasp the gravity of the situation, so I do the only thing my mind can agree with me on at the moment, and I begin peppering every inch of Roman's face in small, salty kisses.

The tears turn to breathless laughter, and when I've probably kissed him as many times as years old he is, I throw my body back into his, wrapping my arms around his neck.

His giant arms wrap around me, and I have never felt more loved and safe in all my life. Scratching the hair on the back of his head, I whisper, "You came for me," and choke on another sob.

His arms hold me harder as he mumbles into the crook of my neck, "I will always come for you." He pauses and pulls away, cupping my cheeks. "For the rest of this existence and every existence we are given, I will come for you. I will find you. I will love you." As tears begin streaming down my cheeks, he gently wipes them away with each of his thumbs as he continues, "No matter the time. No matter our names. No matter the distance. I will come for you, and you will have all of me. Forever."

I'm still crying when he crashes his lips against mine in the kind of kiss that reminds us both that we're still alive. He pulls away before I've had my fill and rests his forehead against mine. Just breathing me in while I do the same, and the tears finally slow to a stop.

I flinch when a cough sounds in the corner, reminding me that there is an entire room full of people.

Looking around me again, the tears I had finally pushed away return with a vengeance when I see them all.

I meet Benny's eyes first, and he cracks me a small smile with just enough sunshine to make me feel better.

Andrei looks the worst, and with an expression I can't decipher, he shakes his head as if trying to chase the somber feeling away before he tries to smile; it really just kind of looks like he needs to take a dump.

The twins are smiling and shoving each other, and Slate offers a clipped nod with the tiniest lift of the right side of his mouth, which I'm pretty sure is a smile.

Miss Tilly and Jeanine hold each other's hands, resting their heads against each other and smiling so big it looks as though it might hurt.

Not one eye in the room is either dry or without dark rings underneath. *Were they all worried about me?*

"I was out of my mind, and none of them were far behind me," Roman replies. Apparently, I said that part out loud.

He looks over my shoulder at everyone with a nod, silently thanking them all for their support, and Lord knows what he's telling them telepathically. *I can't wait until I can do that.*

Benny and Miss Tilly race over and reach me first, crashing into me from either side and sandwiching me in a hug as Roman steps back to make room for them.

Benny snatches me away from her and spins me around the room, yelling, "We're so glad you're okay!" Earning himself a growl from Roman, who snatches me back and carefully sets me on the bed I must have been sleeping on.

Miss Tilly perches herself on the bed next to me, taking my hands in hers, patting and rubbing them softly as she asks, "How are you feeling, my dear?"

I give myself a moment to actually think about my body and take a quick assessment. "I think I'm okay now. Nothing feels wrong anymore. They kept drugging me every time I woke up and tried to think of a way out."

"You were heavily sedated. I was able to give you some medication to help combat the effects on your body and your wolf," Jeanine says softly as she approaches and stands next to her sister.

"When I was there, every time it started to wear off, it took so much effort to wake any small part of my body." Another small sob bubbles past my lips as I turn back to Roman and say, "I thought I would never see you again. I was so scared of what you were going through without me."

And just like that, he's snatching me away from everyone and holding on to me like he'll never release me again. I don't even consider fighting it. I melt into his embrace and soak up everything he's giving me.

Miss Tilly walks around the room, swatting the other men

and chasing them out when Jeanine speaks up once more, "I'm staying here for a while, Luna. Just holler if you need anything."

Andrei is the last to leave. His stare burning into my skin and that strange tugging feeling making me pull my brows together. When we make eye contact, I can almost feel his pain, but also his relief. *Relief that I'm okay?* I give him a small awkward smile, hoping he'll explain the strange look he gets on his face sometimes one day.

When he finally leaves the room, he gently closes the door, giving us a moment to appreciate that I'm still alive and this isn't over.

9
ROMAN

It doesn't matter that she's in my arms; she's breathing. I still can't believe this is real. I made it this time. I wasn't too late.

Now that she's awake, Benny and the twins are headed back to the subdivision to see if they can find out who those men were, why they had Leera, and who they work for. Slate and Andrei are going to check on our guest in the cells that I had built a level beneath our basement, which is the level beneath the garage.

What would I do without my men? For a bunch of strong, immortal werewolves, this tiny little woman in my arms reduces us to whimpering pups when she's not okay. I know I wouldn't have survived losing my mate a second time, and honestly, I don't know how well my men would have fared either.

Jeanine calling her Luna as she left also warmed my heart. My people would finally have the Luna they deserved.

My thoughts continue to plague me of what could have happened if I hadn't made it in time when she turns in my lap, wriggling free to kneel in front of me.

"You got my text," is all she says with glossy eyes.

"I'm so sorry I didn't think to track your watch sooner. I found your phone in my car and was on my way to bring it to you when Zoey…"

"OH MY GOD, ZOEY, is she okay?! They didn't take her too, did they? I didn't see or hear anyone other than me and the two men," she bursts out.

"Hey, shhh. Zoey is okay, though terrified and worried about you. I called to let her know we found you and that you're okay. I told her that I'd have you get a hold of her when you woke." I try to calm her with a low voice and rubbing circles on her wrist with my thumb. I don't want to break the happy cocoon we're in, but I need to see if I can learn anything from what she remembers.

"Sweetheart, can you tell me what happened? What do you remember?" I ask softly.

She lowers her head and begins to fidget but nods. Taking a deep breath and releasing it, she raises her chin until we're once again eye level.

"I had just gotten home, obviously, and when I got to our dorm room, Zo wasn't there. So, I checked the board, and it said she was studying under our tree, and I should join her. I grabbed my schoolwork and changed my clothes before rushing out to join her…except…" she trails off, but I don't push her; I just move my hand to her thigh and continue to draw circles with my thumb.

"As soon as I got back outside, hands seemed to grab me from all over. I didn't even see anyone out there. I tried to scream and fight, but no one was there to see anything. They took my backpack, tossed it on the ground, and threw me in a van. Before I could do anything else, they drugged me, and I blacked out." She looks to me for some kind of mental confirmation, so I give her a small smile and nod, still not interrupting her with my words.

"One of the times that I woke up, I kicked a stool and gave myself away. I don't know how many times they drugged me," she says on a small sniffle and climbs back into my lap.

Now using my hand to rub her back, I urge her to continue, "Did you see them? Hear them? Names? Anything at all?"

"Not really. I never saw them because I couldn't risk them knowing I was awake. The one time I heard them speaking, it sounded like some rich, bossy guy voice, and then the guy that I assume was just in charge of watching and taking me. The rich-sounding guy said they were going to…" Her body begins to tremble, and I wish I didn't need this information so she wouldn't have to go through it. "He said that they were going to dis-p-p-ose of me. He said that I was in the way of something."

She clutches onto my shirt like they're trying to take her all over again. I wrap both arms around her, holding her close again, promising that she's safe. "I've got you, my little miracle; I've got you. I'm so sorry I wasn't there."

"That's…that's all I remember. I was out of it most of the time," she says as she snuggles closer to me.

I continue just holding her and thanking the Goddess that she's okay. "Would you like me to grab your phone so you can text Zoey?" I ask softly. Her only response is a small nod.

I attempt to release her to stand, but she whimpers and clings to me; my heart cracks right down the middle, my wolf snarling at me for upsetting her.

"Leera, baby, look at me," I beg, still cradling her body against mine.

She lifts her chin just enough to bring her icy blue eyes to mine while keeping her tiny body plastered against me.

I gently push a loose lock of silver hair behind her ear as I say, "I wasn't going anywhere. I was just going to grab your phone off the charger in the kitchen for you, but you are more than welcome to hang onto me like a baby koala bear for as long as you like. You'll hear no complaints from me," I finish with a goofy smile.

She smiles and nuzzles into my chest as I stand with her in my arms and make our way to the empty kitchen to fetch her phone.

Just as I unplug it from Slate's charger, a gasp comes from my right, and I whip my body to face the owner with fire in my eyes.

10
Leera

You've got to be fucking kidding me!

India stands in the entryway, her name-brand purse on the floor by her feet, and her arms crossed against her plastic chest. If looks could kill, I'd be so fucking dead, but so would she, because Roman looks like he might literally kill her right now.

"India. What. Are. You. Doing. Here?" Roman asks slowly.

"I...I...well, you didn't call me after our talk," she sputters before smirking at me.

My stomach bottoms out as the jealousy starts swimming through my veins. I struggle to remove myself from his body, but he squeezes me once. I look into his eyes and see a silent request to listen. I nod, but I still climb out of his arms to stand at his side.

It's now that I realize I'm standing here in nothing but one of Roman's hockey shirts and a pair of fuzzy pink socks. I internally face palm myself, while on the outside I'm standing tall.

Her furious eyes bounce back and forth between Roman

and I before she smirks, taps her fake nails on her still crossed arms, and speaks again, "Roman, darling, I came by to set up a meeting with the King to discuss our succession to the throne."

She's pleased by my sharp intake of breath, but it doesn't last when her eyes move to Roman, and she doesn't miss his body vibrating with barely controlled rage.

His arm pulls me even tighter to his side. I instinctively lay my hand over his heart and look up to smile at him, trying to calm him and his wolf. He looks down, and the rage visibly bleeds from his face.

"I'm here," I whisper, patting my hand on his chest. He smiles that smile that takes my breath away, brings his other hand to stop my patting, and holds our hands to his heart.

With his smile still on his face, he turns his attention back to the seething woman standing before us as he says, "India, I specifically told you I would call you when we could speak. I was busy and unable to reach you yet. However, as you decided to barge into my home where you're not welcome anymore, I suppose we can just do this now."

His gaze grows distant for a short moment, and I know he just gave the men a heads up that this is happening now.

Nodding to himself, he continues, "I'm not marrying you, India."

My jaw drops at his blunt declaration, and she begins to stomp towards us but only makes it two steps before a growl rips from Roman as he drops the real bomb.

"Leera is my mate."

The fire that courses through my body as he claims me in front of her is very inappropriate, but I kind of love it.

India's arms have dropped to her sides, and she's panting.

Now she's the one barely hanging onto her anger, but he's not done yet.

"The Goddess has returned my mate to me and given us another chance in this lifetime. I won't be marrying you, and if that's a dealbreaker with the King, I won't be taking the throne. I don't care."

India is fuming, and I'm honestly surprised there isn't literal steam coming from her ears and nose when she takes one more step towards us, pointing her finger at Roman and then me. "You know what? Fine! I don't need you to be a queen. Keep the little bitch. You don't get a second mate, so keep lying. You'll regret it when you're bored with her and come crawling back to me, and I'll no longer need you."

She's only just gotten the words out of her mouth when Andrei walks through the door. He instantly takes on a lethally calm presence I've never felt before. With a murderous look on his face, he snatches her overpriced purse off the floor with one hand, using his other hand to gesture towards the door.

"It's time to go, India. Now," Andrei growls.

She crosses her arms again, stomps her foot, and seems to plant herself where she stands. He takes a single step to close the final distance between them and levels her with a look that rivals Roman's anger.

"Last warning. Leave on your own will, or I will remove you from this house."

She turns her head away from him, and I shit you not, she puts her nose up in the air.

He looks to Roman for approval, and when he confirms with a small nod, Andrei loosely grabs her by her wrist, still being careful not to harm or bruise her because he's apparently a gentleman, to a fault. He lightly tugs her towards the door, offering her one more chance to leave on her own.

She continues to try and pull her arm back and stay in the townhouse. She begins kicking and seething, and Andrei has no choice but to drag her towards the door and literally throw her out because she still refuses to leave.

When the door finally slams shut, I know I shouldn't be so happy about the scene that just unfolded in front of me, but I am, and I don't care.

Roman finally claimed me as his mate to the queen of putrid, bitches! I startle when I feel what must be my wolf, and a small squeal escapes me.

Andrei is walking back towards us, and even he's finally smiling.

Both men look at me at once with eyes full of happiness, and Roman explains, "We can feel your wolf. Can you feel her?"

"I just did! If I had to explain it, I'd say she was happy, like she…like she was prancing around, I think."

Both men continue to beam at me until I snuggle back into Roman and meet his eyes. "That's the first person outside of… us"—I wave my arms around between us and his men—"that you've told I was your mate." I'm so happy I can't stand it. It's at that moment my body decides to remind me that I was just kidnapped and drugged for Goddess knows how long, and my knees give out.

Roman captures me quickly before I hit the floor, setting me back on my feet and holding me against him.

"That's enough excitement for you. You need to rest," he mumbles into my neck as he nuzzles me and inhales a deep breath.

"It was totally worth it." I release a happy sigh and look at Andrei and say, "Thanks for throwing out the trash."

We all erupt into laughter for a moment before Serious Andrei makes a swift return. "What are we going to do about her? You know she'll go straight to the advisor."

Roman becomes serious while he thinks, all laughter forgotten. "We'll figure it out. We always do. But it had to be done."

I just nod, trying not to think about all the shit that's going to hit the fan.

Roman speaks again, "Sweetheart, how about you grab your phone and we'll go upstairs and sit under your twinkle lights, and I'll call Benny to grab some dinner? What would you like to eat?"

"Oh, I'm starving. Can I have a big greasy cheeseburger with onion rings and a cookies and cream shake?"

Roman just looks at me like I hung the moon when he says, "I'd hand you the heart in my chest if you asked for it. I'll have Benny get your food. Grab your phone."

As soon as my phone is in my hands, he scoops me back up into his arms, and we head upstairs.

11
India

Each ring of the phone in my ear pisses me off even more until he finally answers. "You fucked up!" I screech.

"Stop acting like a banshee and explain why you're having a temper tantrum, India."

I can't help but laugh. "You don't know, do you?"

His silence causes me to laugh even harder.

"Care to elaborate what it is you're on about?"

"You failed again, and we won't get another chance, Avram."

"I said, what is it you're on about? I'm growing irritated."

"I said you failed! He has her. Roman has the girl. And better yet, he says she's his mate!" I scream into the phone.

"I figured she might be when I stopped by the house and realized she carried the same scent as the first peasant. Elaborate on what you mean by he has her? I was just at the house yesterday."

"What the fuck else could I mean when I say he has her, you pompous ass?! He has her. In his arms. Right. Now. I was just there to try and get closer to him in his time of need, and you fucked it all up again!"

My Pucking Family

My lips pull into a feral grin when he roars into the phone as I hang up to let him stew in his failure.

12
ROMAN

After finally dealing with India—the way I should have a long time ago—we all ate dinner together on the roof. When I asked Benny to bring Leera and me some food, I didn't expect him to show up hauling multiple bags of food with everyone on his heels. We sat under the twinkle lights that she loves so much and had a meal together…like a family…because she's finally *home.* Here with me, where she belongs. It may take her longer to get there, but it's only home when she's here. My men feel it too. The way her being here just makes everything feel right. Complete.

This is my family, and I'll do anything to protect them. I would take on the Gaoddess herself if she tried to take her from me again or take any of them.

We finished eating a while ago, and the men took the trash downstairs and went to take care of their own business. We've just been sitting here in comfortable silence ever since, appreciating the moment while she texts with Zoey.

Leera shivers, and I realize that she's still just wearing my t-shirt and socks.

"Alright, time to go in. I saw that shiver," I announce.

"You've been keeping me warm this whole time. It was just a little shiver," she pouts.

I scoop her into my arms and make my way towards the stairs. "How about a bubble bath?"

Her eyes light up, and she melts into me. "Ugh, that sounds like heaven," she groans, and I will my body to ignore it.

I figured she'd like to wash the experience off and come out feeling refreshed. Still holding her, I navigate the stairs and halls until I reach my room—our room—and lay her on the bed while I prepare her bath.

After Leera's first overnight visit, I asked Matilda to stock my bathroom with girly things she might want or need. I even picked out a few things that were recommended on Pinterest again. She's loved everything I found on there so far.

I rummage through the cabinets, and once I find everything I want, I set it all on the counter. I light a few candles, placing them around the tub. I fill the tub with skin-melting hot water—her exact words—and add some calming chamomile and lavender bubble bath for her.

While it's filling up, I arrange a bunch of other chick shit along the counter for when she's finished: some weird little pink things that say they're eye masks, a strange, handheld machine that says it's a facial massager, honeysuckle body lotion, a clean pair of fuzzy pink socks, three different kinds of panties to choose from so she's comfortable, and another one of my t-shirts.

When I return to the room, she's right where I left her. "Are you okay to get in by yourself or do you need my help?"

"I think I can manage on my own," she blushes.

I promised her that we would take this slow, and knowing that I won't be able to keep my hands off her if I stay, I walk downstairs, letting her enjoy the bath on her own. Making my way to the kitchen island—our unofficial meeting place—I catch up with the guys about India, hockey, and Leera.

I knew it was risky admitting who Leera is to me, especially to India, but it had to be done. She can't keep barging into my life, thinking she can get her way.

Now we have to be prepared for the potential retaliation, and I am *not* ready to think about how fast this will reach my father. But he will have to face the truth as well.

"As far as Leera's safety is concerned, I'm going to try to convince her to switch to online classes and move in with us," I say as the men shoot skeptical looks at each other, avoiding eye contact with me. "I know she's going to fight me on this, but she just won't be safe on that campus, and you all know it."

They collectively nod, and Benny adds, "It could help if you reach out to her favorite professor and let her know that Leera can complete all her assignments surrounding the team this semester, if she needs to."

"That's not a bad idea at all. If I can get her core class to cooperate with me on this, she would be more likely to go along with it," I agree, rubbing my jaw in thought.

"She won't be happy about leaving Zoey," Slate points out.

"You're right, she won't, but she won't be a prisoner here. She can still go do things with someone watching from afar, and Zoey can come over any time she wants," I grumble, trying to convince myself more than anything.

All I want to do is go to her dorm room right now, pack up all her things, and move her into our home where she'll be safe, but I already know if I don't talk to her about it first, she won't take the news very well. We're mates, and she's still making me court her. Not that I mind. I get to learn all about her while making her happy; it's just not how it usually works, and my wolf was on edge before she was kidnapped.

I'll just have to do my best to convince her to move in with me so that I don't have to make an ass of myself and do it anyway.

Will she want to stay with me in my room? *Our* room. If not, we still have plenty of space. She can have her own room to do whatever she wants with. Until I've convinced her to stay with me anyway.

Bringing the conversation back to getting everything taken care of, I say, "Okay, so we took care of that one away game, we have a home game tomorrow and the rescheduled away game on Thursday…" I pause, tapping my fingers to the counter, elongating one claw to tap as well.

Andrei is the first to break the silence when he says, "If she agrees to take her classes online, I don't think we'll have a problem getting her to agree to travel with us for games."

"And why the hell would I be taking my classes online?" she snaps from the hallway.

Shit.

I cross the space to go to her, but she's already in a battle stance. She rips the weird pink things off from under her eyes, plants her fuzzy-pink-socked feet apart, locks her hands on her hips, and presses her lips in a thin line.

At least she seems to have enjoyed the things I laid out for her. I wonder which underwear she chose…nope, not the time.

I turn to my men for help, but Benny just smiles and shakes

his head, the twins look to be taking bets, Slate's just smirking, and Andrei looks like a kid who got caught with his hand in the cookie jar.

"Hey, Sweetheart, did you have a good bath?" I ask calmly.

"Don't Sweetheart me, Roman. I asked you a question."

Shit.

"I was waiting for you to finish your bath to talk to you, but we wanted to discuss some safety options for you moving forward."

"Don't drag us into this just because you're in trouble," Benny pipes up with that stupid shit-eating grin on his face. It pisses me off even more when I catch Leera trying not to smile at him, and I'm not able to catch the small growl that escapes me.

Benny places his hands up in surrender and backs away.

Leera's icy-blue eyes sharpen and return to me. "Let's hear it then," she says as she crosses her arms over her chest, not realizing she's only made it harder for me to focus with her breasts shoved up like that.

Groaning and scrubbing my hands on my face, I take a step back to sit on one of the barstools, hoping to make myself less demanding. "Leera, baby, you are my number one priority. Now and for the rest of my life. Do you understand that?"

She narrows her eyes and nods, not speaking.

"You were kidnapped, and I couldn't protect you," I add. "I can't…" I choke on my words, and my men filter out of the room.

"I can't lose you. I can't do it again. I won't survive it." My voice drops along with my head. "Without you, I will burn every world to the ground before following you to the afterlife, Leera."

I hear her small body approach me before she throws herself

around me. "I'm here, Roman. I'm here because you found me. Because you saved me," she says with her sweet voice as she lifts my eyes to hers. They're no longer ready for war.

"But you were taken because of me. You were in danger because of me."

"Don't give yourself so much credit, Big Guy. The only people responsible for what happened to me are the people that took me and the snobby, rich dude that hired them," she says with absolute certainty.

"And I understand you want to protect me, but it's the twenty-first century; you don't get to make all the plans for my life behind my back. If we're going to be partners, I want us to be equals. We do things and discuss things, especially the hard things, together."

"Yes, ma'am," I respond with snark in my tone, causing her to swat at my arm.

"Alright, seriously though, what were you guys talking about?" she asks, serious again.

"We were hoping to convince you to change your classes to online..."

Her eyebrows scrunch together.

"...move in with us where it's safe..."

Her head tilts to the left just slightly.

"...and go with us to all of our away games," I finally finish.

She stands there for a minute just shaking her head before she says, "Roman, I understand you're worried, but I'm still going to school; I'm not moving in with you yet, and I might go to away games." The only thing she didn't do was stomp her foot.

Rolling my head around my neck on a sigh, I continue trying to convince her to no avail.

Izzy Elliott

"Look, I'm done talking about this. I will be fine. It's late. Do you want to spend some actual time together before I have to go to get ready for tomorrow, or do you just want to take me home?" she asks, leaving no room for further discussion.

I shouldn't have pushed so hard, but how the fuck am I going to be able to do anything other than fucking follow her around to make sure she's safe?

That's it! We have a home game tomorrow. I don't need to practice. I can follow her around all day, make sure she's safe, and then take her to the game with me.

"Okay, okay, you're right. I'm sorry. We can talk about this more later. Did you get enough to eat, or do you want to grab something else before I take you home?"

She looks at me suspiciously at my sudden relent but nods. "I'm still a little hungry."

"I know just the spot. We can just lounge on the couch until you're ready to go?" I offer.

Slate, do we have any tiny GPS trackers I can use? I ask through our mind link.

Yeah, let me go find one.

I'll be with her, but I will feel better if we have another level of safety for her.

We don't even turn on the TV when we plop onto the couch together. She's still texting Zoey a mile a minute. I pull her into my side, tracing circles on her thigh until she's ready to grab a quick bite and head back to her dorm.

13
Leera

Dinner was so good, oh my gosh! We went to this little family diner that only had like seven tables, and I had the best shredded Rueben sandwich I've ever tasted.

We're pulling up to the dorms now as my heart starts trying to pound its way out of my chest. I grip my legs so hard that my knuckles turn white. I'm begging the panic to spare me, but it's not. I can feel the wave of anxiety cresting through my body. I already know it's going to drown me.

I have been working so hard to stay strong and show everyone that I can handle this. I want to be strong, but it's so fucking hard. I want to prove to Roman that I am okay. I don't want them to worry about me because that just draws more attention. If I can pretend that I'm strong enough to get through this, no one will give that sad look that makes me feel pathetic. Like the looks I got when Mom and Dad died.

A small, broken sob bubbles out of my throat and before I can process what's happening, I'm being pulled from the car. I start beating my hands on anything I can reach.

Giant arms close around my body and lower me to the ground, and my initial reaction is to keep fighting, keep screaming, anything to get away. I can't let them take me again. I don't want to be drugged again. I'm about to scream when...my body recognizes him before my mind does.

Roman.

I was in the car with Roman.

Roman pulled me out of the car.

Roman is holding me tightly to his body to calm the flood of despair.

Roman let me beat on him without a care.

When my mind finally reaches all the same conclusions as my body, I'm unable to control the way my body trembles, releasing the adrenaline it had prepared to fight my way out. My wolf and I just whimper, which only causes him to hold me even tighter.

"It's okay, my little miracle. It's just me. I've got you. Always. I've got you," he continues his mantra, while he rocks my body and rubs my back.

I'm thankful it's already dark outside and few people, if any, would have seen my panic attack.

When I've finally calmed enough to stand, he closes the car doors and walks me into my dorm building. All eyes are on me, which means they all know what happened. Or they think they do anyway.

The second I open the door to our room, Zoey comes barreling into me hard enough that I would have fallen to the ground if Roman wasn't supporting us.

I don't even have a moment to say anything before Zoey bursts into tears, and I have no choice but to follow her. Roman shuffles us far enough into the room so that he can close the door, granting us privacy, and just stands guard while we let it all out.

When I've cried all I want, I look from him to Zoey and say, "I think...I think I'm okay from here. Thank you."

He's definitely not happy about my dismissal, but he nods anyway and lowers himself to kiss the top of my head, holding it for three Mississippi's before he slowly walks out of the room, leaving Zoey and I to have some time to talk about everything that happened.

When the door closes, I rush over to lock it. With Roman gone, it immediately feels colder. I'd be lying if I said I wasn't considering calling him back to come get me. I feel like I left one of my limbs with him. Will it always feel like this when I'm away from him, or is it because of the abduction?

With my wolf growing stronger—*that's still so weird to even think about*—so is the mate bond between Roman and me. The previously light tugging feeling between us has grown into more of a magnetic-pulling feeling that's becoming increasingly hard to ignore.

I make my way back to Zoey, and we curl up in her bed and talk. I tell her about everything that happened, minus the wolfie stuff, and I must still be in shock because, while my nerves are running high, I'm not a hysterical mess like they are in movies. *Is this what disassociating feels like?*

I just want to go back to pretending to be a normal college girl, trying to have a normal college girl experience.

We order some comfort donuts to be delivered since I already had a second dinner with Roman.

I only eat one donut, severely overestimating my stomach's

capacity for food. We eat in peaceful silence, just cherishing each other's company. When Zoey finishes her donuts, she turns on the live-action Cinderella to watch. Not the Disney one. The one with Brandy and Whitney Houston.

We stay snuggled in her bed until I feel like I can't keep my eyes open any longer. My phone pings across the room, so I pull myself from the warm blankets to check it.

> My Pucking Mate
>
> Goodnight, Beautiful. Let me know if you need anything at all. I'll be there ASAP. Sweet dreams.

Smiling to myself, I text him back before crawling back into Zoey's bed to sleep near someone. I don't want to be alone. I finally drift off to sleep with Brandy singing about her own little corner and her own little chair.

14
ROMAN

In order to keep the peace, I allow Leera to believe that I'm giving her the independence she so desperately wanted, but with her being kidnapped, there's just no way in hell I'm leaving her alone.

I will not lose her again. Not now. Not ever.

So I'll grant her the illusion of my submission for now, unless something causes me to show myself.

I make myself comfortable in my car, parked with a direct line of sight to the main door of her dorm building. Benny is stationed at the other end of the building. At the only other door out of her building.

We'll be tired tomorrow, but for my mate to be safe, being tired feels like a very small payment to make. Andrei, Slate, and the twins all offered to take shifts, but I refuse to leave. I can't. Benny also declined and vowed to stay in position.

Thinking of how easily she allowed herself to smile at dinner, having been kidnapped mere days ago. I know she's strong, but she thinks being strong means doing everything on your own. It doesn't have to be that way, but it seems that's a lesson she'll have to learn on her own over time. I am proud of her tenacity to overcome this, though. Some people allow themselves to wallow in the fear, but you have to find a way to keep going or it will drown you.

Thankfully she wasn't harmed, and, because of the drugs, she slept nearly the entirety of her captivity. In our short amount of time together, I had already noticed she struggled with some panic and anxiety before all of this happened. The last thing I want is for those to worsen.

I can also feel her wolf growing stronger. I still can't get a solid read on her, and neither can my wolf, but Leera can feel her so much more now, and that will allow them to finally connect as well. I know my wolf can't wait to be reunited with his mate.

He chooses that moment to huff in agreement, and I smile.

I've been without Imogen for five hundred years, but it makes me wonder how many lifetimes we've had together.

Our bodies, and the bodies of our wolves, can change from life cycle to life cycle, but our souls will always recognize each other.

How many lives have we lived together?
How old are our souls?
How long between lifetimes do we have to wait to find one another again?

I allow my thoughts to carry me away while keeping my eyes trained on the door.

Checking the time, I see it's nearing ten o'clock. Being right here all evening, I allowed Leera some space and didn't text or call her. I would have responded if she initiated, but I wanted to make sure she had all the time she needed to decompress with her best friend. If hers is anything like mine, they're also good for the soul.

I pick up my phone, shooting her a quick text just so she doesn't think I've forgotten about her.

> Goodnight, Beautiful. Let me know if you need anything at all. I'll be there ASAP. Sweet dreams.

Benny, how are you doing over there? I ask, checking in.

Living the dream! I can hear the sarcastic smile in his voice before he continues. *But really, Boss, everything is fine.*

Nodding to myself, I settle in for a long night when Benny pipes back up, *Hey, Boss?*

Mhmm?

What's the plan for tomorrow?

You and the others will go to the rink to practice like normal, and I'll be with Leera.

What are you going to do if she catches you following her?

Beg for forgiveness. It's all I can do. I won't be sorry for making sure she's okay.

His only response this time is a snort.

I wasn't lying when I said that Leera made it hard to care about anything anymore. I still don't know what I'll do about away games if she doesn't agree to come with me. It's just all too much to try and figure out right now. So, I'll just take everything one day at a time until we get it all figured out.

15
Leera

I wake with a start when I hear a crashing sound. My heart is hammering in my chest, and my body is on high alert when Zoey pokes her head out of our bathroom with a guilty smile. "Sorry about that; I dropped my curling iron."

Taking a deep breath and nodding, I reply, "It's okay, just a little jumpy. I guess that's to be expected."

She takes a step into our living space with a sad smile on her face. "Are you sure you're up for this? You know you can always take a week off or switch to online classes for a semester."

My eyebrows draw together, and I become immediately defensive, "I am not switching to online classes. I'm fine, and you know how badly I just want a normal college experience. Can't we just pretend none of it ever happened?"

"Do you think you can do that?" she asks me, slightly tilting her head to the side.

Crossing my arms over my chest, I offer only a strong nod and eye contact, hoping I relay how determined I am to really do this. She seems to accept it and shrugs her way back into the bathroom to finish getting ready for classes.

I growl a little and drag myself out of bed when there's a knock at the door. My body decides to lock up, and I just stare at the door.

You're supposed to choose fight or flight, not freeze, I scold myself.

"Zoey, can you get that?"

She comes bouncing out of the bathroom, and when she takes in the state of me and offers another sad smile. She checks the peep hole, shrugs, and opens the door.

She leans out the doorway, holding the door open with her leg, and returns with a coffee in each hand. There's also a bouquet of flowers tucked between her body and her elbow. The flowers are powder pink and look like they're climbing up the stem. I immediately melt because I know exactly who left these.

"At least he remembered my coffee order," Zoey mumbles with an ornery grin.

I can't help the smile that spreads across my face at this sweet man of mine.

Mine? Hmm. That's the first time I've thought that to myself, and I can't argue with how right it feels. I take a sip of my coffee, snatch the note from the flowers and swoon.

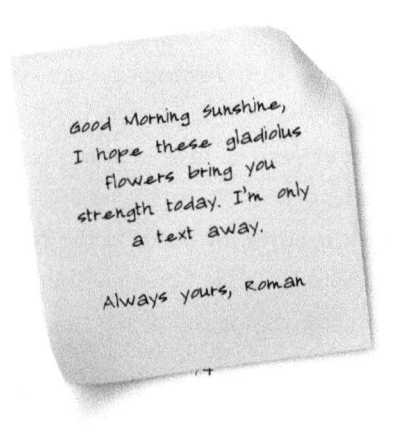

> Good Morning Sunshine,
> I hope these gladiolus Flowers bring you strength today. I'm only a text away.
>
> Always yours, Roman

I take the flowers and set them on the table by the window, raising the blinds so they can get plenty of sunshine for the day. At that moment, someone walks by our ground-floor window, causing me to screech and jump back.

Zoey comes barreling right back out of the bathroom. "What? What? What?!" she gasps.

"I'm sorry. Someone walked by the window when I opened the blinds. It startled me is all. I'm okay."

She crosses the space between us and hugs me, not letting go until I do, then looks me straight in the eye. "You're not accepting defeat or something crazy if you *need* to take online classes to get through the semester, Lee. Shit happens. Okay? I know you want to be strong, but it doesn't make you weak not to torture yourself. Just…just think about it, okay?" she finishes with a soft smile.

I just nod.

Maybe this will be harder than I thought.

This is definitely harder than I thought it would be. I'm only in my second class of the day, with two more to go, and I've already had fifty miniature heart attacks for no reason whatsoever. Every unexpected sound is making me jump. The guy behind me sneezed a minute ago, and I thought I was going to pee my pants. It also doesn't help that word spread like wildfire that I'd been kidnapped, and everyone has been pointing and whispering at me all day. It's kind of hard to blend in with the silver hair and all. I can't decide if the attention or the fear is worse, but they're both so suffocating.

I guess sometimes, no matter how hard you want something, you also have to admit that you might not be able to do it, and it looks like I likely won't be able to handle the normal college experience that I wanted so badly. At least not right now.

Trying to focus on the rest of the lecture while also coming to terms with that realization is hard.

Okay, so I might need to take classes online, then what?

Do I live on campus and stay in my room by myself while Zoey goes to class like a normal person? Or do I take the next step towards crazy and move in with Roman and the guys? Like recently finding out I was a freaking werewolf wasn't enough, let's see what else she can handle. *UGH, this is all just too much.*

Apparently raging and ranting at myself is exactly what I needed, because before I realize it, class is over. I've got forty-five minutes before my Photojournalism class with Professor Sinclair. I'll go talk to her and get her opinion on my situation.

I do my best to slink through the halls to her classroom, trying to attract the least amount of attention. When I finally reach the right room, I open the door just enough to squeeze through and collapse against it once it clicks shut.

Professor Sinclair looks up from her papers; she seems to be grading. She obviously wasn't expecting it to be me as she lurches from her seat and moves unnaturally fast across the large room to meet me.

"Oh my gosh, Leera, I'm so glad you're alright!" She seems to almost choke up. "Can I touch you?"

All I can do is take deep breaths and nod.

Her hands come down on my arms, moving up and down in a reassuring way, but it doesn't feel anywhere near the relief I get from Roman's touch.

"Are you okay? Do you want to talk about what happened?" she asks, turning back to her calm and kind self.

"Kind of...to both," I say quietly, trying to keep the tears in.

She just nods, causing her tightly-coiled natural hair to bob a little, then gently walks me to a chair.

"Is it okay with you if I just get it all out as quickly as I can?" I ask her. "I'm afraid if I stop, I'll break down and won't be able to get it all out."

"Of course, whatever you need."

I start from the very beginning and tell her about everything with me and Roman, filling in more human-related issues where the werewolf details would be. Her eyes continue to grow as I carry on, and the rich ebony skin on her forehead wrinkles as she takes in all the information that I'm throwing at her.

"And now I'm here, blabbing my life story to my professor because I don't have anyone, and I don't know what to do." And with that, the dam breaks and the sobs escape me.

"Oh, honey, shhhh." She wraps me in a small hug and pats my back. "Why don't we go back to my office, so we're not in a public room, and we can talk through this, and I can just give my next class direction? Everything is going to be okay."

I nod slightly as she stands and heads to her desk to gather her things while I try to gather myself to make it back out in that hallway.

When Professor Sinclair is ready to go, she seems to mumble something under her breath before she opens the door, and goosebumps prick at my arms.

I brace myself for all the attention I've been getting today as we join the masses and walk towards her office. I have my arms wrapped around myself, watching my feet hit the floor as I try to avoid the curious glances and whispers, but I don't feel the intensity of attention on my skin like I had the rest of the day.

I sneak a peek around, and I'm just moving through the crowd unnoticed. It's not that I'm not grateful, but I wasn't even able to go to the bathroom earlier without some girls trying to ask me questions. I'm thankful for whatever is happening, but it's also kind of weird. I quickly lower my head to keep watching my shoes and enjoy the brief lapse in everyone's curiosity and scuttle along next to Professor.

My mind cannot even process the fact that we made it all the way to her office without a single incident, but I'm not about to start complaining.

I pile all the stuff beside the seat in front of her large, walnut desk before allowing myself to plop into the chair, resting my elbows on my knees, and hanging my head in defeat.

The sounds of Professor Sinclair moving around the room before taking a seat at her desk help to calm my frayed nerves. She allows me a few more moments of silence, and then she breaks it, jumping right back into the fire and saying, "Leera, let's start with what do you want?" she asks, emphasizing the word you.

I open my mouth to offer my immediate answer, but close it and allow myself to really consider the question.

After a few moments of thought, I reply, "I want to be a photojournalist like my parents. I want to be with Roman without complications. I just want to be a normal college kid, and I really couldn't be farther from it at this point." Another small whimper threatens to escape, but I manage to hold it in.

Her chin rests on her steepled fingers while she considers my response. The gold rings she wears on every finger glisten in the harsh lights above us.

She reclines, her back resting against her chair, as she seems to contemplate the best way to move the conversation forward.

"I understand your drive to have the 'normal college experience,'" she emphasizes with air quotes. "But you could ask fifty kids what they think a normal college experience is, and you could potentially get fifty different answers. Some people can get an entire degree online without ever stepping foot on a campus, while others may never take an online class. For some people, college is about education only, and there is no room for friendships or relationships, while other people make bonds that last a lifetime. There are even people who never wanted to go to college but are forced or feel obligated, so they're just getting through it."

I nod along as she speaks because she's absolutely right. I hadn't thought about it that way. *But where is she going with this?*

"I think there might be a little more that you're not telling me, and surprisingly enough, I think I understand what you can't tell me, and I want you to know—she's cut off by a thunderous knock on her office door.

My initial instinct is to cower, but my body relaxes without any instruction from my brain. *That doesn't make any sense; why would Roman be here?*

Just as the thought crosses my mind, I'm enveloped in the scent of cherries and leather, and for the first time today, I'm at peace…even if it only lasts a moment.

16
ROMAN

I'm on my way to Professor Sinclair's office to talk to her about Leera's potential online class situation when I pick up Leera's honeysuckle and spun sugar scent going in the same direction. Except...shaking my head, I try to clear the negative thoughts; I'm just rattled from everything going on.

But when I reach the door to her office, the instinct is overwhelming, and I have to calm my wolf snarling just under the surface.

I knock on the door, hard enough to rattle it, and gather a little attention. *Shit.* I paste on my magazine smile with a small wave, and while I still have their attention, I no longer smell the fear that had started to permeate the air.

The door opens only a crack, revealing that the professor and my mate are both in there, and I now know that my instincts were not wrong.

"Well, hello, Roman. Leera and I were just discussing—"

Allowing a little bit of my wolf through the surface for her to feel, I interrupt the professor, "I think you should ask me to come in so we can have a very detailed discussion about what's going on here."

To my surprise, Sinclair smiles sweetly, nods, and opens the door enough to allow my entry into the room. Leera looks confused, but once the initial shock of my arrival wears off, she's scrambling off her chair and into my embrace.

I barely wrap my arms around her when the flood gates open and she allows herself to break. I scoop her into my arms and make my way to her discarded chair to sit and calm her so we can have a much-needed conversation.

Professor Sinclair is waiting patiently in her seat, grading papers until we're ready. Her calm patience raises more questions than I already had when I came down the hallway.

There's no way Leera knows who she is.

When a small hiccup escapes my little mate, I smooth her hair away and hold a kiss to her forehead. When I feel her muscles relax against mine, I rest my forehead against hers. "Leera, I know you've been through so much lately, Sunshine, but we're about to have another big conversation, okay?"

Her icy blue eyes meet my green and blue ones, then widen as she processes what I've said.

"I came here to discuss your learning situation with Professor Sinclair. You've spoken so fondly of her; I knew if anyone could help you understand online classes aren't bad, it would be her..." I take a moment and try to arrange my words to have the least impact.

"It seems as though a new conversation with your favorite teacher is needed," I say to Leera, but my eyes find Sinclair's, who offers a smile and a nod.

"I completely agree, Roman. Leera has just filled me in on

a lot in my classroom, and we came here to have a more private conversation. First, I would like to calm Leera's worry and let her know that I can recognize you as mates, so that fills in a lot of the less understanding portions of her explanation of the situation," she finishes with a comforting smile towards Leera, whose mouth has fallen completely open.

"H-how could you possibly know... wait—are you a werewolf?!" she all but screeches at her favorite professor.

"No, she's not. That's why I came here as quickly as I could. Leera, she's a witch. I smelled your scents on the way to the office, and I could feel the magic." Turning my head back to Sinclair, I snarl, "What did you do to her?"

She just nods for a moment and clasps her hands together before explaining, "Yes, Roman, I am a witch, but I am not a dark witch, so you and your wolf can calm down."

Yeah, right.

"The magic you felt in Leera's scent in the hallway was only a cloak. She's had a very hard day with the amount of unwanted attention she's received, so I simply brought her to my office undetected by the others in the hallways."

This time when Leera's mouth falls open, her whole head tips forward, and she's just looking at Sinclair in shock. "Y-you're a witch?"

Again, Sinclair just smiles and nods.

At first, I was enraged to have a witch around Leera, but there's something about her...I think I trust her. My wolf confirmed she isn't a dark witch. They have a rotten tone to their scent that only our wolves can detect, unless they're so evil that the smell of rot can be sensed without our wolves confirmation.

As my brain rifles through the information I have about

Leera, it hits me like a train. "Her parents were witches."

It's not a question. I already know the answer, but Leera doesn't. She's frantically looking between Sinclair and me. When she finally lands on Sinclair, she's gifted another smile and nod.

Answers are overwhelming right now, though, and I can feel her panic and anxiety rising. I mold her body to mine as tight as I can get it while trying to soothe her.

After a moment, she's calmed enough that the anger is winning the war within her body, and she flies off my lap, pointing a sharp pink fingernail at Sinclair. "Why does everyone know so much more about my own life than I do?! You knew, didn't you? You knew I was a wolf? You knew my parents were witches! Why was I left in the dark? To live a lie for my entire life?!"

Her pain is shooting through the room like daggers, and I feel every hit like a physical blow. My wolf tries to push through my skin to protect and comfort her, but I hold him back as best as I can.

She's not in danger. I've got this. She's just feeling a lot right now.

At that, the professor raises both of her hands in front of her to show that she is surrendering, stands from her desk, and walks over to Leera. Tentatively, she takes Leera's hands in her own and kneels in front of her, urging Leera to sit.

"Sweet girl, I didn't know how much you knew. Your parents planned to tell you everything before you came here. I didn't know if they had had the opportunity before you lost them. Unfortunately, I don't have all the answers you seek, but I'll answer any of them the best I can, and I'll start by telling you that yes, I knew. Yes, I knew you were a wolf. Yes, I knew they were witches, as am I. You weren't told as a child to protect you. They never even told us from what, so that I cannot share. They demanded that you be kept safe, at all costs."

Tears slowly trickle down Leera's cheeks.

"Is that why they p-poisoned me my whole life?" she asks quietly.

Sinclair at least has the decency to look ashamed. "We tried to find another way, but it was the only way to keep your wolf from presenting herself. They said no one could know."

My thoughts continue to tumble around in my brain, trying to piece all of this together.

"If they wouldn't tell anyone what they were protecting her from, how is anyone supposed to know now that they're gone?" I ask, trying not to bark at her in irritation.

"I wish I knew. They said it was to protect all three of our realms, but that's all I know."

I rear back with the magnitude of those implications. "When you say all three, you mean Zabella, Earth, and Sabbax?"

She nods grimly in response.

"What's Sabbax?" Leera asks quietly.

"Sabbax is the witch's realm. Like the werewolves have Zabella and humans have Earth. Each paranormal being has their own realm populated with only their kind and their mates. Others can cross and visit and such, but it takes special approval to be accepted within another realm," I try to explain as clearly as I can.

"So, like when we, I mean humans, try to move to another country?" Her nose scrunches as she tries to piece everything together.

"Yes, Sunshine, much like that."

"Wait, why is me being safe so important?"

Sinclair and I exchange a glance that says neither of us know how to answer that question.

"It looks like we don't know yet, Sweetheart, but I promise we'll find out." Sinclair nods in agreement.

Men. We have more research to do. I'll catch you up when we get home.

"Alright, let's return to the topic of Leera's academics. She very badly wants to stay in class, but I was tryi—"

"Actually, Roman," Leera interrupts me with a hand on my arm. "I've had a really rough day, and I have to admit, you were right. Professor Sinclair helped me reframe the way I was thinking about everything. It's not what I wanted, and it's not what I thought my normal college experience would look like, but I think it's best for now. Especially while we figure out what the hell is going on with everything."

I nod and use all the physical willpower that I have not to break into a grin and whoop out loud. I'll be able to keep her safe this way.

Before I can even ask, she looks at me and says, "We'll talk about the rest later." This time, I do smile.

"Well, I'll leave you two to it then. And, Leera," she says with a sweet, motherly smile on her face. "Now that we share some secrets, please call me Willa."

The smile on Leera's face almost seems to glow with the new addition to her small group of people in her life.

I collect her things from the floor, and we're about to walk out the door of Sinclair's office when she asks, "The small cloaking spell will have worn off by now; would you like another one to get you out of here?"

Leera seems to consider this for only a moment before straightening her back and standing as tall as her four-foot-eleven-inch frame will allow. "No, thank you, Prof…Willa." She smiles, turning her gorgeous face to mine, and places her hand around my forearm. "I've got Roman I'll be fine."

17
Leera

As if I didn't draw enough attention to myself all on my own, walking through a crowded college building with a hockey god's arm draped around my shoulder was definitely the cherry on top.

The guys are all sputtering in awe, and the chicks are divided between jealousy and thirst, if you catch my drift.

I just focus on the tingles and warmth radiating from where he touches me as we move through the seas of people parting for us.

For the first time today, I feel a genuine smile bloom on my face when I realize that Roman didn't even seem to notice anyone else that was in the building. Sure, he does the dude nod thing to some of the young men praying for his attention, but when he sees the women who would happily take my place on his arm, he either leans over to kiss the side of my head or pulls me closer.

No matter what happens, for once, I feel like it really will be okay. Life is different when you know you have a seven-hundred-something-year-old werewolf, hockey god for a mate. And this is only the beginning.

I never have to feel alone again. I think as my eyes try to fill with tears. This immediately alerts my wolf and Roman to my feelings, but I just smile and nod.

When we finally reach our car, because he drove it again today, I slide into the seat with my name embroidered in pink thread and release a heavy breath. All the weight I've been holding on my shoulders all day finally evaporates.

When Roman makes it into his seat and starts the car, I turn to him with a guilty smile and say, "Go ahead and say you told me so."

He just shakes his head and says, "I didn't want to be right about this one, Sunshine. I know how much it means to you. That's why I went to talk to Sinclair. To make sure you can still have as much of the experience as you can handle."

I turn to just nod again when I release another loaded sigh. "When will I stop learning new things about my parents...and myself? When can I just be Leera and live that normal life I wanted?"

This time he throws his head back and laughs, causing me to cross my arms and scowl at him. "And what exactly is so funny?"

"Baby, I hate to break it to you, but *normal* is long gone. You're a werewolf. Your mate is an NHL player. Your favorite teacher is a witch," he says each one while counting his fingers to drive it home. "I'm afraid that ship has sailed."

And damn him if he's not right.

Things could easily be worse, though, even when you throw the kidnapping situation into the mix. I could hate my college roommate, hate college, not have Roman. The last one causes my wolf to whine a little.

"So, where are we going then?" I ask since we're just sitting in the car.

"That's up to you. Do you want to go to your dorm to get some things and come home with me, or what's the plan?"

I drop all the way into my seat and stare at nothing through the windshield while I really think about what I want.

Do I want to stay with Zoey and be away from Roman?

Do I want to move in with Roman and miss Zoey?

Do I want to keep trying to pretend that I'm normal and my entire life isn't different than it was months ago when I thought I had my new life all planned out?

Roman waits patiently, allowing me all the time I need to sort through my thoughts until I finally have a line on a tentative plan.

"How about a trial run?" I finally ask, and the look on his face tells me everything I need to know. This won't be a trial run. This will be forever. But he doesn't have to know that yet.

"Of course, what are you thinking?"

"I'm thinking I'm going to run in there and get some essentials and some clothes, and leave a note for Zoey to call me so I can tell her what's going on. Is that okay?"

"It's more than okay," he says softly and lovingly. He tucks an errant strand of my silver hair behind my ear before he leans forward and kisses me on the forehead.

He drives me over to the dorm building and walks me to my dorm room. He let me know he was going to give me some space to do what I needed, and he'll be waiting for me in the car. I ping around the room in a tizzy, grabbing everything I know I'll need and a few things I might.

After writing Zoey a note, I place my hands on my hips and look around the little space that's brought me so much happiness. I'm not happy that I'll likely be leaving here, but it's time to keep moving forward.

With a couple of bags, I make my way down the hallway. When Roman sees me lugging around my stuff, he dashes out of the car and snatches all the bags from me and carries them to the car.

I can't believe I'm really doing this.

The whole way to his townhouse, he's holding my leg and rubbing it with his thumb, and it's making me feel all kinds of needy things only he's ever made me feel. *Is this normal? For my body to try and take over my mind? Why's it so hot in here?* His touch feels so good, but this time it's igniting more than our usual tingles. This feels too intense. What if something's wrong again?

18
ROMAN

I still can't believe she agreed to stay with me, even if it's just as a trial run. I thought it would take much more work. I had speeches planned. It's going to be incredible to get to know her at a new level. Not just on dates, through text messages, or in passing. I finally get to learn who Leera is all the time, and when she thinks no one is looking…because I'll always be looking.

I'm lost in my happy trail of thoughts when the scent of her arousal begins to drown me. It's heady and intoxicating, but it's not just that. I can sense her anxiety rising again.

"Leera, honey, what's wrong?"

Her cheeks turn pink. She tries to just smile and shake her head like she's fine.

We're almost home now, just another minute. Her scent is so strong I have to roll the car window down to be able to drive and keep my wolf from ripping through my skin.

How can this be? As I ask myself that question, my wolf begins to howl beneath my skin. *How the fuck am I going to handle this?!* This is the absolute last thing I would have thought we'd be dealing with today.

"Leera, look at me. Are you okay? Do you feel feverish?" I ask, but I already know the answer. Between her scent strangling me and the frantic look on her face, I already know. Her whole body is blushing a rosy-red color; it really can't be anything else.

She's starting to squirm and whimper in her seat when we turn onto our street.

"Let's get you inside, and I'll help, okay?" I ask, hoping I'm getting through the panic and need.

She barely nods.

Benny, Slate, Andrei, Dolos, and Eris out. Go find something to do until I let you know. I brought Leera home, but I think she's going into her first heat. Matilda, Meredith, and Jeanine, if you could please stay in case she needs you?

I hope I sound strong because I'm trying to keep my shit together here. If she'd been raised a werewolf, she would have been taught about her heat and how to handle it.

Instead, I have to help her navigate through it while also finding a way to help her without crossing the lines that she's laid down. I worry she'll be so lost in her heat that she'll forget her wishes. I won't be the bad guy. I can't let that happen.

We pull into the garage. The men took off in wolf form to go check on the pack, and they won't be back until I give the all clear. We don't know how long this will last. Some can be as short as twenty-four hours, while others can last a week. The thought of this lasting a week has me groaning while my dick involuntarily raises his head to volunteer. *Sorry, buddy, you'll probably be sitting this one out.*

I rush out of the car, going around to the passenger side to gather Leera in my arms. I'll come back for her things later. The second her body is pressed up against mine, she begins to mewl in a need she doesn't understand.

"Roman, wh-what's wrong with me? I feel so…" she shakes her head like she's trying to clear her mind.

"Let me get you inside, and I'll take care of you, Sweetheart." I didn't mean for that to sound as husky as it did, but my wolf is riding me hard.

As soon as the elevator reaches the main floor, I fly through the space to my room as quickly as I can. It's probably only been two or three minutes, but with her panting and fidgeting like this, it feels like forever.

I kick the door shut behind us and lay her on the bed. I intend to step back, but her hands grab a hold of me and pull me on top of her in an earth-shattering kiss. *Kisses are allowed.* I remind myself as I soak in the taste of her. Honeysuckle and spun sugar so sweet I could easily have her for dessert for the rest of my existence. When she releases a deep moan, I gently break the kiss and rest my forehead on hers.

"Leera, baby, can you hear me?" I ask as I place one hand on each side of her head, so that she'll make eye contact with me. Very hooded, heavily glazed eye contact, but it's the best we've got right now.

"Baby, this is called your heat. I know you photographed animals with your parents. Are you familiar with animals in heat?"

The haze seems to lighten its grip on her for the moment, and I can see the wheels turning in her head before she squeaks out, "I, uh, y-yeah, I remember."

"Werewolf women go into heat when they meet their mate. Since your wolf hasn't been released yet, I didn't even think about this. I'm so sorry, Sunshine."

"Is that why I feel, why I feel so…" she trails off and scoffs, running a hand down her face, clearly embarrassed.

"Hey, none of that. This is completely natural, and you never have to feel that way with me. We'll get you through it. Normally, the only way to help with the needy feelings you're having is by mating." Her eyes widen, and for a second, and I worry she might bolt, so I rush to finish my sentence, "But I know you're not ready for that."

She visibly relaxes, but I can see the lustful glaze recapturing her eyes.

"Baby, focus I need to know what you want me to do. I want to help, but I don't want you to feel like I'm taking advantage of you," I ask quickly, worried that we didn't get to discuss this before it happened.

She nods, sits up, and slowly crawls around me to the edge of the bed. She pushes me down on the bed where I was leaned over to talk to her. She, even more slowly, lifts her perfect little body over mine until she's straddling me and there's no way she can't feel how this is affecting me.

"Leera, I…" She stops me with her finger on my lips.

She replaces her finger with small kisses across my lips, moving towards my jaw.

When she gets to my jaw, she finally starts to speak, each word separated by a kiss along my stubbled jaw line, "I. Trust. You. Roman. Please. Take. Care. Of. Me." Her last words end on another kiss that takes my breath away. I don't know if it's the kiss or the trust that she's granted me, but my heart feels light and my dick feels heavy. Her scent filling my room. Her need rubbing along mine. It's the perfect storm, and if I don't keep my shit together, I'll jeopardize the trust she's placed in me.

I allow her to kiss me until she's moaning and whimpering through the kisses. I don't know what the heat feels like, but from the descriptions I've been told, it feels like you'll never be able to cool down again. All while the need inside you consumes all logical thoughts or actions. The longer you go without release, it can turn painful, and I don't want her to experience that.

When I pull away from the kiss, I scoop her up in my arms and lay her in the center of the bed and growl, "Let me make you feel better."

19
Leera

*R*oman.
    Roman.
Roman.

All I can think, or feel, or see right now is him.

I'm laying on his bed staring up at him, panting with a need that I can't even explain. It literally feels like if he doesn't touch me…there, I might die.

No one's ever touched me like I want him to touch me. I tried a few times, but it just never felt right. I didn't know what I was doing, and I was usually in a tiny apartment or tent with my parents. That would have been just weird.

I can see the hungry look in his eyes, and still, I trust him.

I can feel another wave of heat rolling over my body and can't help myself when I arch my back, whimpering and wriggling on the bed, and my mouth decides it also doesn't need my consent. "Please, Roman. Please touch me."

He growls and rolls his neck before taking his shirt off.

I scramble back up to kneel next to him so I can touch him.

I want to feel him, and, *GOD, he feels so good.*

He snatches my hands gently and lays me back on the bed and says, "Let me make you feel better. I need my control, and if you keep touching me like that, I won't have any left."

If he thought that would help, he was wrong. It's only made me hotter and more breathless.

He leans over me, and this time he kisses me. He kisses me like he needs my kisses to survive. Like he could live off of just me.

Then his hand is slowly trailing up my thigh. When he reaches my waist, he slips his hand beneath my shirt and continues moving north with featherlight touches. When his fingers barely skim across my bra line, my breath hitches.

"Are you okay?" he asks with worry in his eyes.

At first, I can only nod, but he seems to be waiting for me to speak. "Yes, yes, yes. I'm more than okay," I ramble as I sit up and pull my shirt off.

His hungry eyes turn completely to molten desire, and the power I have over this monster of a man urges me on. I reach forward and trail my fingers across the ripples of muscles on his chest before I bring my hands behind me to unclasp my bra and gently toss it off the side of the bed.

Roman looks between my chest and my eyes, like he's not sure how to proceed without crossing the line of my wishes, so I reach across the small space between us, take his hand in mine, and slowly bring it to my breast.

The second his hand engulfs me, my head falls back. The tingling and sensations flying through my body are otherworldly. I never want this feeling to stop. He brings his other hand up to my other breast, and the intensity of it causes me to moan, and for once, I can't find an ounce of embarrassment.

His lips trail kisses along my neck and shoulder, nipping and almost whining when he reaches the soft skin in the bend of my neck. His hands begin to knead my breast and nipples, and I gasp at the change in the already intense feelings. I swear, there is literal lava collecting between my thighs.

He continues his exploration of the top half of my body, and I feel like I'm being worshipped and torn apart all at the same time.

His kisses leave my neck and skitter across my collarbone. He continues kissing his way down my body until he's eye level with my chest. I'm wriggling and panting and holding on to him for dear life when he makes eye contact with me, and so incredibly slowly, let's his tongue fall out of his mouth. Maintaining eye contact, he leans farther forward and uses his tongue to trace circles around my nipple, and this time, it's me who growls.

The heat in my body continues to rise, and I feel like I'm losing my mind, but oh, what a way to go. I feel like fire is dancing through my veins, and I've never felt as treasured as I do in this moment with him. My mate.

My fingers instinctually tangle in his hair and hold him to me while he sweetly tortures each breast.

He finally pulls back to look into my eyes again, and the green and blue hues of his eyes almost seem to be glowing.

"P-please. I need…" *I don't know what I need, but I just know I NEEEEEED it.*

"I know, baby. I know. Are you sure you're comfortable?"

"Yes. Please. Help. Touch me," I beg.

He leans back into my body, kissing a path down my sides and around my belly button before continuing across my waistband, making eye contact again as if asking for permission.

Instead of answering him, I reach down and shimmy myself loose from the black joggers I wore to class today. He takes a deep breath through his nose, growls, and rolls his neck again before laying his body beside mine on his massive bed.

I begin to whine and protest because I want, no need, his attention where the liquid fire continues to collect, but he silences me for a moment with another blistering kiss.

Each kiss I've had with him grows stronger, more urgent, more life-altering. This one is no different. Our bare skin connected from the waist up is causing my brain to misfire. All there is in this moment is me and him. I notice even his normal cherry and leather smell has gotten stronger and a bit—how do I explain it—muskier?

While his lips devour mine, his fingers are again trailing my body, and all I can do is hold onto him. When he reaches the edges of my pink lace thong, my hips take on a mind of their own and lift into the pressure of him, and I moan.

He slips his fingers lower, still outside of my panties, and he's almost where my body is screaming with need. When his fingers connect with a bundle of nerves, I cry out, causing him to groan, and I can feel his need for me against my hip.

He rubs his fingers around the sensitive spot, and I swear, my very existence is coming unraveled. I don't know what to do with my hands; they're frantically touching him everywhere I can reach. My hips won't rest on the bed, begging him to keep going.

He breaks our kiss, and now all I can hear is my moaning whimpers and his growly, labored breathing. He bends himself over me, taking one of my still tender nipples in his mouth, twirling his tongue around it while his fingers are on the move again, retreating further south.

When he reaches the sodden pink lace separating us, I throw my head back and moan his name.

That seems to be the key to unlocking a little bit of my mate's control, because once he has a hold of the flimsy material separating us, he says, "I'll buy you all the pretty little underthings your heart desires, but these are mine now." With those words, the tip of his finger elongates into a claw. He flicks his wrist, cutting the lace from my body, and brings it to his face as he closes his eyes and inhales.

"What are you doing?" I gasp, the embarrassment trying to weasel it's way back in.

"The scent of your need for me is..." His eyes open wide, and I can feel the heat radiating from them as they dart to meet mine. "It's intoxicating," he growls, tucking the stolen garment into his back pocket.

I'm completely bare to him. No one has seen me naked for years. My parents stopped helping me bathe over a decade ago. I've always been modest. I thought I would feel more vulnerable than I do in this moment, but all I feel is cherished. How could I feel anything else with the look on his face? He seems to be cataloging every inch of my skin. Committing it all to memory.

When another surge of heat rolls through my body, he's not even touching me when I cry out. It immediately shakes him from his thoughts and brings him back to me. He's tracing all the same pathways he did before he touched me the first time, but now, instead of being lust drunk to his kiss, I want to watch. I want to see how he touches me while I feel it. So I prop myself up on my elbows as he reaches where my panty line used to lay.

He stops again, making eye contact and silently begging for permission, and fuck if I don't love him for respecting my earlier established boundaries.

Do I love him? The thought causes me to release another moan. *Even if I do, I'm not ready to tell him, but I hope he can see in my eyes what I'm not ready to admit.*

He looks away from me, also watching where he's touching me. Like he wants to memorize these moments too. His fingers finally drift across my smooth skin. I've always hated my own body hair, so action or not, I kept up with the landscaping.

When he finally separates my tender flesh and makes full contact with that same small bundle of nerves, I see stars. "More. Oh, shit. Please, Roman. I need more," I beg shamelessly, and again, I've found another key to unlocking any reservations he may still hold.

"Okay, Sunshine. I've got you."

His fingers twirl around that sweet spot, massaging me in the most euphoric way. When he moves to my core, wet and waiting for him, I suck in a lungful of air. I watch him ever so slowly move his fingers through my folds, collecting the lava my body has only ever produced for him.

When I think he'll finally slide his finger inside of me, he brings it to his lips and licks all of me off of him before bringing it back down. He again collects the wetness, but this time my wish is granted.

He slowly runs his finger along my opening before barely sliding it inside of me, and I immediately know that this is what my body wants. I need this. I need him.

"Roman. Now. Please," I pant out, and he slides it a little farther inside, and my head falls back.

"Good girl," he breathes while he allows me a moment to adjust to the size of his finger while I moan. When I bring my head back up to meet his eyes, I nod my head and he moves.

When he moves like that, the rest of the world completely falls away. There's no bed. No room. No house. There is only Roman and I.

"Yes. Yes. Please."

"Are you ready, baby?" he asks, and all I can do is frantically nod my head.

He brings his other hand around, so his forearm is laying up my stomach and across my belly button. While the first hand slowly moves his finger in and out of me, stopping just as he meets the resistance of my innocence. His second hand finds that beautiful bundle and rubs it in small circles while he continues to move inside of me, and I feel like I'm being shot into the stratosphere.

I can't breathe. I can't speak. Whatever this is just keeps growing and climbing, and if I'm being honest, it's a little scary.

"I'm here, Leera. I've got you. Fall. I swear, I'll always catch you."

The sincerity in his words is the final push my body needs, and all of a sudden, an explosion goes off inside of me. The world around me shatters completely as I scream his name and fireworks go off behind my eyelids.

I think I blacked out for a minute because when I open my eyes, he's scooped my body into a cradled position and is nuzzling the crook of my neck, whispering the sweetest words.

"You did so good, baby. Such a good girl for me."

My body is still quivering and fluttery as I allow my eyes to close and take in the moment.

No wonder people are obsessed with sex. If that's what first and second base feel like!

The burning need and desire seem to have tampered down a bit and are no longer bordering on painful.

When I open my eyes to meet his, I see nothing but love in his eyes.

I release a heavy sigh, and he leans in to kiss me on my forehead. Reaching up, I run my fingers up the side of his face and into his hair. Just holding him. Feeling him.

"That was incredible," I whisper to Roman and myself.

"Did it help? Do you feel better?" he asks, returning to his adorable worrisomeness.

I nod, feeling my cheeks heat when I smile and ask, "Can we do that again?" Before I know it, he's flipping and hovering over me again, causing me to giggle.

I don't know how many times it takes before the burning need from the heat is totally drowned in orgasms, but as I drift off to sleep in his arms, I think maybe going into heat isn't such a bad thing.

20
ROMAN

Holy. Fucking. Hell.

Leera drifted off to sleep probably thirty minutes ago, and I'm just laying here staring at her in disbelief.

This still doesn't feel real.

I keep replaying the way her body felt beneath my fingers. The sounds she made. The way she responded to my touch. The way she screamed my name.

Over and over and over again.

I came in my pants. Twice. Like a fucking pup.

But it was worth it. To watch her experience everything for the first time. To be that for her.

Forever.

After allowing myself a few more minutes of watching her dream, I allow my mind to shut down and follow her into sleep.

The sun slipping between the curtain and the wall right

against my eyeball wakes me from the deepest sleep I've had in, well…since the last time Leera stayed the night.

I move to pull her closer to me when I realize I've got my arm wrapped around a Leera-sized pillow lump and not the soft skin of my little mate.

Panic consumes me as I fly out of bed and search for her. I follow her scent into the bathroom, but she's not there either.

I barrel out of the room and down the hall, following her scent in an increasingly frenzied state, when I bring myself to a screeching halt.

Her silver hair is tied up in a messy mass on top of her head, and she's standing in the kitchen in nothing but one of my hockey tees.

The worry melts away, and my dick takes notice as I sneak up behind her without making a sound. I notice she's humming as she sways her hips back and forth while she makes something on the stove. I have to bite my knuckles to keep from growling and ruining my surprise appearance.

When I think I've got myself together, I take another step forward. Her body seems to notice my presence before her mind does. Her body visibly melts into me as I grab her hips and pull her towards me, gently kissing her from her shoulder to her ear.

She squeals in surprise; the sound also going straight to my needy member. She twirls around to face me, laying her hands on my bare chest. On instinct, I grab onto the back of her thighs, lifting her against my body. I take a couple of steps towards the counter, gently settling her adorable ass on the cool marble, choosing this moment to capture her mouth with mine. She melts even further into me, clutching my waist, pulling my body closer to hers.

She's the one who pulls away slowly and rests her forehead on my chest before panting, "I wanted to make us breakfast," she says in the softest, sweetest voice I've ever heard.

"You scared me," I admit, and I hold onto her tighter. "When I woke without you, I feared the worst," I finish, dropping my head to the crook of her neck.

She lightly pushes me away from her, capturing my face in both of her soft hands, and says, "Roman Razboinic, you are stuck with me. I'm not going anywhere," she scolds while her eyes volley back and forth between mine.

I nod and pull her to me, smothering her in a hug, while I inhale her scent and the smell of something slightly burning—

"Oh, no! The pancakes!" she exclaims as she shoves me backwards, hops back down to the floor, and returns her attention to the stove.

I chuckle and head over to the coffee machine to find a couple of stranded mugs, some water, and the coffee strewn about the counter as if she wanted to make it herself but didn't know how to use the machine. If I'm being honest, I didn't either when Benny brought it home. He had to teach the twins and me how to use it.

I set about making my little miracle some coffee that I know she wants badly, and when it's ready, I bring the steaming and full mug over to her as I sip on mine.

The smile that lights up her face is totally worth her not knowing how to use the coffee machine. I'll have to remember to tell everyone not to teach her so I can make it for her. Hopefully every day…forever.

I set myself on a barstool across from the stove and just watch her work. Bopping around, completely in her element.

"Where's Matilda?" I ask when I realize she's usually always busy with something in the kitchen.

"Oh." She blushes. "I hope you don't mind. I sent her and her sister to find something fun to do today. I wanted to make us breakfast and spend time together. Maybe try to have a normal day," she finishes with a laugh and another sip of coffee.

"That sounds perfect. We don't have another game until Thursday, so we have time to figure things out," I return with a smile.

We finish breakfast and spend the day together. Just Roman and Leera. She stays in my t-shirt. I stay in my joggers. We watch movies and order food. We ask each other questions and talk about our lives.

Now I understand why humans do this. This social convention of doing nothing together. I've learned so much about her today.

We didn't jump into the plans. We'll tackle the hard stuff tomorrow. Today, we were just us.

As the sky begins to darken, the guys come barreling through the front door because Leera demanded I allow them to come back home.

Benny makes a beeline for her, with that stupid shit-eating grin on his face, and pulls her into a hug. "Thank you for letting us come home, Luna. We know it was you. He would have kept us locked out forever."

With a growl, I pull her from his embrace and back into mine while she giggle-snorts and swats at me, mumbling something about an overbearing alpha before she returns her attention to Benny. "Why did you call me Luna?"

"Oh, sorry," he starts, rubbing the back of his neck. "Since

Roman is our Alpha, his mate is our Luna," he explains.

I can see the wheels turning in her head already. "It's not something you need to worry about. Being a Luna is as much or as little as you want it to be, and we can add it to our list of tasks to work through," I finish with a smile.

She nods and turns to the rest of the men. "Sorry, he kicked all of you out because of me."

Andrei speaks before anyone else can, "We don't mind. Really."

He's so short and awkward with her; I'll have to figure out what that's all about too.

Slate just nods and claims his barstool at the end of the island and buries his head in his laptop, hopefully still digging into any connections between India and my father, as well as who took Leera.

The twins plop down on the couch and are arguing over what to watch.

I turn back to Leera to find her taking everyone in with that sweet and soft smile, and my heart just continues to soften.

"Roman, do you know what I did with my phone? I want to add everyone's numbers to my phone so I have them in case of emergencies, or if you end up kicking them out of the house." The ornery twinkle in her eyes makes me want to kick them out all over again.

"I don't remember where you left it, but you start looking, and I'll grab my phone to call it." I call back to her over my shoulder as I walk towards the kitchen while she dismantled the couch cushions.

While I hit the call button, her phone immediately starts ringing from the other side of the kitchen, and a surprised laugh escapes me, much louder than I would have expected.

Everyone's attention turns to me when I hold up Leera's phone for everyone to see, one eyebrow lifted in question to Leera.

She bolts towards me, giggling, when she snatches the phone and holds it to her heart. "I didn't know what to put for your contact name, so I decided to have some fun with it!"

The men are all laughing with us now, and it takes a solid seven minutes for us to get it out of our system. Leera straightens, having doubled over in laughter, and is now wiping tears from her eyes.

I lean forward to plant a kiss on her forehead. "I love it."

The blinding smile I'm rewarded with could stop my heart.

"Men, grab your phones and text Leera's number with your names, so she has them all."

They all pull out their barely used phones, and her phone slowly starts pinging with all the messages, and she's furiously typing as she adds them all to her phone.

Now that that's taken care of, we resume our restful evening, and I'm once again struck with the realization that everything just feels right when she's here with us.

21
Leera

I can't decide whether falling asleep or waking up in Roman's arms is my favorite. As I lay here, currently cocooned in his embrace, I think about the whirlwind of the last few days.

That heat. *Whew.* We've shared a few more steamy kisses, but we haven't had anymore physical interactions since it faded. My brain is happy with myself for setting boundaries and thankful that he is taking them seriously for me. My body and my heart are mad at my brain and worry that maybe it wasn't as good for him since he hasn't tried to engage in more.

The day after my heat was peaceful normalcy and gave me an unexpected glimpse of what my life moving forward could look like with Roman.

That next day was a little less lighthearted. After Roman brought me breakfast and coffee in bed, complete with a small bouquet of wildflowers, we put on some fresh lounge clothes, sat down, and really discussed everything going on in my life. All the things I kept tabling for later because I wasn't ready to deal with them. I wasn't ready to discuss them because having to sit down and talk about something made it a real, living, breathing thing that could hurt you, but it couldn't be delayed any longer.

Roman and I had set up our own little war room in the living room to make sure we had enough space to map out and discuss everything we needed to tackle.

First on the list was my schooling and living situations. We agreed that I would take my classes online for the rest of the semester. It wasn't worth going through the turmoil of attending physical classes if I couldn't enjoy them. At the end of the semester, I would re-evaluate how I felt about everything and go from there.

As far as the living situation, my head and heart were in substantial disagreement.

My head kept saying: It's too soon to live with him; I want to be a strong and independent woman; I will miss Zoey; and I want a normal college experience.

My heart and wolf were adamant about it not being too soon because we're mates and usually once two people mate, they move in together immediately; I can still be a strong and somewhat independent woman while living with my mate; Zoey can come visit and stay the night with me any time, and really, my normal college experience flew out the window a long time ago.

So I did what any eighteen-year-old girl going through a new life crisis would do. I excused myself to one of the guest bedrooms and texted my best friend.

> SOS

> 911
>
> I'm okay, but like I need you.
>
> Your thoughts and opinions.

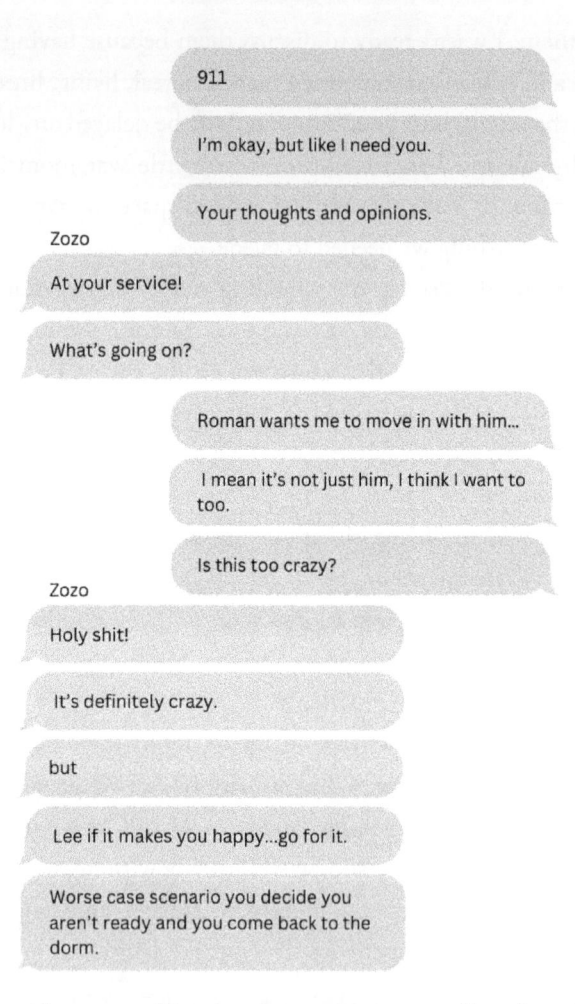

Zozo

> At your service!
>
> What's going on?

> Roman wants me to move in with him...
>
> I mean it's not just him, I think I want to too.
>
> Is this too crazy?

Zozo

> Holy shit!
>
> It's definitely crazy.
>
> but
>
> Lee if it makes you happy...go for it.
>
> Worse case scenario you decide you aren't ready and you come back to the dorm.

I smile to myself at the supportive nature of my best friend and send up more thanks to the universe for bringing her to me.

> If I do this...
>
> Will you come stay the night so we can have bestie time?

> Maybe like once a week or something?

Zozo
> DUH!
> You're stuck with me bish.
> Forever.

Happy tears filled my eyes.

> Thank you Zo.

I clutched my phone to my chest and took a moment in private to let the conversation wash over me.

I was really going to move in with Roman.

My soul mate.

Well, at least the moment was mostly private; my wolf purred in agreement.

Once I had allowed myself to completely absorb my decision, I quietly left the guest room. As I padded down the hallway, I found Roman pacing the living room with one hand tangled in his hair. I hadn't meant to worry him. I had wanted to sneak up on him, like he had done with me the morning before, but he almost immediately noticed my presence and turned to make eye contact with me.

Unable to say the words out loud, I let myself smile as I felt heat rising to my cheeks and nodded at him. His happiness was palpable as he scooped me into his arms and held my body against his.

"Please say that nod meant you decided to live here with me. Not just because you feel that you need to, but that you want to," he pleaded with his chin resting on top of my head.

I leaned my body away from his so that I could look into his eyes as I told him, "Oh, Roman, I want to live here, with you, because of you," I finished with my hand pressed against his heart, earning me another panty-melting kiss.

When Roman pulled away, I wasn't able to capture the whimper that escaped my lips at the loss of his touch. He gently stroked the side of my face with his chin while he said, "There will be plenty of time for that later, but if we don't finish working on our list, I will soon become much too distracted, and we won't get any more work done today."

While my body very much wanted to spend the rest of the day distracted with him, he was right. This all needed to be discussed, and any plans needed to be decided upon.

We moved on to the next item. Family. There was almost too much here to unpack.

At the highest level, my parents were witches; Khaos is kind of my soul's brother; and who were my real parents?

Learning that my parents were witches probably should have been more of a shock than it was, but after everything I've been through in the last couple of months, it's easier to just roll with the punches. Even though it was kind of startling to hear that my parents were witches, some things just made sense. The biggest one being the wolfsbane.

My parents hadn't *poisoned* me my whole life out of some kind of darkness. They were trying to protect me from something. Though it would have been helpful to know what that something was.

Some other things that just seem to make sense now that I know they were witches are little things from my childhood.

Getting so close to animals during a shoot, and them never even flinching at our proximity. The few times they identified a strain of plant life thought to be extinct.

Witches or not, the love was real. I know that with the same fierceness that I know Roman is my mate. I just wish they had trusted me to keep their secret. Hell, I wish they'd told me my own secret.

Even though I find myself wishing a lot of things with them had gone differently, I am grateful that this new life brought me to Willa. While unorthodox, it's comforting to have another person in my life that I can completely be myself with. It kills me to hide so much of myself from Zoey.

As far as Khaos being the brother to my soul's previous life…that one feels a bit more precarious. I wasn't sure I wanted a relationship with him or not. I could feel the bond between us, but how would he react? Would he be angry with me for the reincarnation of his sister that was outside of my control? Would he try to keep me from Roman? Would he even believe me? Roman suggests that I wait and see what happens the next time I have any interaction with him and go from there.

Back to the topic of parents: I hadn't even thought of who my actual parents might be. When Roman brought it up, I was in a state of shock for a few moments. I knew my parents were witches, yet I hadn't put the puzzle pieces together to wonder if I had other parents out there. God, that's so weird to think about. The thought of two people, or in this case werewolves, being the ones who brought me into this world and not the people who raised me.

I was honest with Roman when I let him know that I wasn't ready to try and find out who they were right now. It's just way too overwhelming.

Since the men hadn't found any leads about the kidnapping and weren't able to get anything out of the man who they had found in that house with me, the trail had gone cold for now.

During our discussions of family, I had a moment of peace wash over me when I realized that even though I lost my parents and have mystery parents out there in the universe somewhere, I still found the most amazing little family. Zoey, Willa, Roman, Benny, Slate, Dolos, Eris, and even Andrei have all become my family.

I also used that moment to have a little more fun than our strict get-shit-done day had planned, and I started a group text.

My Pucking Family

> I'm sure you're all wondering why I've gathered you here today.

> LOL just kidding, but seriously tho, until I have the awesome telepathic connection thingy, I want us to have somewhere to talk if that's okay. 😊

My Pucking Mate

> I should have expected this.

Benny

> Hell yea!

Andrei

> This is also a good security feature.

My Pucking Mate

> Explain.

Andrei

> If she needs anything and one of us isn't available, she only has to send one text and we'll all get it.

> **Eris:** This isn't supposed to be security related.
>
> **Dolos:** Oh this is gonna be fun.
>
> **Slate:** Right you are brother.
>
> Make sure everyone updates their settings to allow notifications from this group text at all times.
>
> **My Pucking Mate:** I said not security related.
>
> We promise it won't be only security but you can argue the benefits.
>
> Whatever back to work.

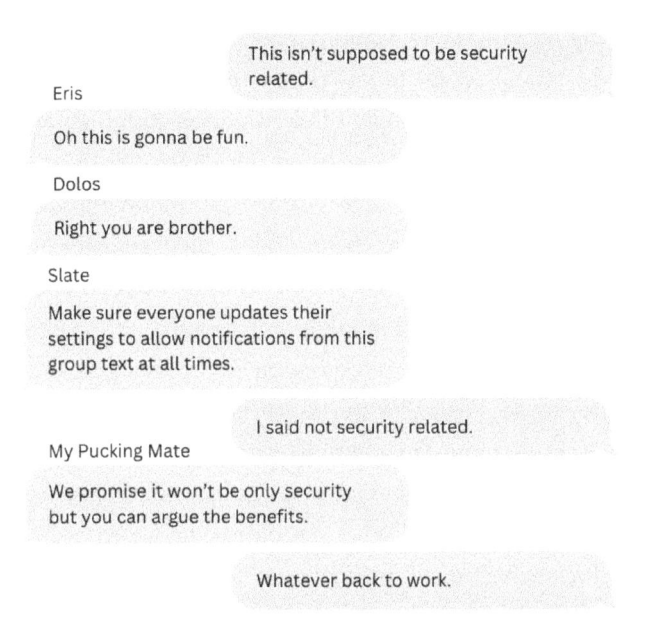

After that, we discussed hockey and how I would fit into their schedules. I would obviously be at all home games with Zoey, and there would be a guard stationed nearby, just in case. During practices I would usually be home—*it's still strange to think of this as my home now*—working on my school work, but will be free to do whatever I want. It was the away games that worried Roman the most, especially since he had one in three days.

With the league being inherently werewolf, there are policies in place for mates. Those policies grant me access to anywhere the team goes. As much as my old, independent tendencies scream at me to resist and say that I can take care of myself, I just don't really want to. I don't want to be away from Roman anymore than he wants to be away from me. I don't want to watch him play on the television when I could be in the stands cheering for him. Why wouldn't I take advantage of everything in place that allows me to stay close to my mate?

That left the only topic of conversation to be me and my wolf. I luckily hadn't had anymore incidents of her trying to unnaturally force a shift, but with the full moon approaching, there is an especially good chance that I will experience my first shift very soon. When I say approaching, I mean according to my web browser, the full moon is in five days.

I try not to freak myself out with all the thoughts and concerns trying to plague my mind. I really do. But after the first episode, I can admit I'm afraid. Even though every time I think about it, my wolf does that calming cat-like rub against my skin to make me feel better. When I'm not being afraid of my first shift, I'm so excited. I'll finally get to meet my wolf. What will she look like? How will it feel to be covered in fur and run on four legs?

Roman said that the evening of the full moon, we can go to the pack and join the others who will be experiencing their first shifts. He said the whole community comes together around a big bonfire and supports the pups through their first transition. Even though I'm not a pup, I still feel the urge to take part in the traditional rite of passage among my own kind. I also want to meet the pack. They will be part of my family and my new life.

As much as I dreaded really working through everything, it was unexpectedly cathartic to lay it all out there and have plans in place.

My thoughts are pulled back to now, when the tree trunk of a man behind me grumbles incoherently into my hair. I wriggle in his hold until I've turned myself around to look at him, brushing the sandy hair from his face. When his eyes finally open and meet mine, I'm once again rendered breathless. The happier he is, the brighter the green and blue of his eyes are, and right now, the most talented painters in the world couldn't capture the emotion shining there for me. For little, boring, orphan Leera.

Only, I'm not that girl anymore. I'm a werewolf. I'm someone's mate. I have a best friend. I'm a college student with a witch for a professor. I'll never allow myself to take this life for granted ever again.

"Why do you think so loudly, so early?" he grumbles.

It would seem my mate is also not a morning person. The thought causes a small giggle to squeak out.

"I've just been going over everything again from the last few days," I reply, snuggling into his embrace when I feel him harden against me.

The liquid fire spreads through my veins again, but it's not the burning and desperate need that it was when I was in heat. I'm still in control of myself.

Roman shifts and groans, "Sunshine, you're going to have to stop rubbing against me like that. I'm trying to behave for you."

I do as he says and stop wiggling. I, however, have no interest in behaving this morning. I play with a few of the hairs on his chest before I trace his ab muscles leading to the perfectly defined v-muscle and allow my fingers to skitter across the waistband of his boxers.

I watch my fingers as they explore his body when he lightly grips my chin to look at him.

"You don't have any idea how amazing this feels, but you don't have to do this if you aren't ready yet." It seems to pain him to say.

We're lying on our sides facing each other, so I take his hand from my chin and lay it on his side before pushing him onto his back. I don't straddle him this time, but I lean over the top of his body and kiss my way up to his face.

"You'll never know how much it means to me that you're keeping yourself aware of my boundaries and limits, but I think it's time you stop worrying about that."

He goes to say something, but I stop him with a kiss that makes me wet.

"I'll let you know if I start to think we're going too far, but that's not what's happening today."

He quirks an eyebrow at me while I return to kissing down his body.

"Last time, you got to explore me." I stop kissing to look him in the eyes when I finish, "And now, if you don't mind, I'd like to explore my mate."

He growls, and the vibrations travel to all the sensitive nerve endings in my body, causing me to release a small whimper.

"Can I touch you, too?" he pleads.

"You can touch but not pleasurably." I smile. "At least until I've finished my exploration."

"Alright, my little miracle, I'm all yours."

22
ROMAN

Waking up and having her here is a blessing that will take centuries for me to believe is real, and that was before she informed me that she'd like to start her day by exploring my body.

Goddess, help me.

Everywhere her little fingers and luscious lips touch feels like it's on fire. Though at this rate, I would happily burn for her.

When she reaches the waistband of my shorts again, she continues to go lower, touching me just over the material, just as I did her.

The difference is that I was familiar with the female anatomy, which makes me wonder, "Have you ever seen a man?" I ask lightly, making sure not to sound judgmental.

She blushes and shakes her head.

"Do you want me to show you or do you want to do it yourself?"

She thinks for a moment and shakes her head again. "This is my time to learn your body," she says strongly.

I pull her to me and kiss her hard for just a few more moments, while also pulling us towards the headboard so that I can lean against it. I want to watch her and touch her while she has her way with me.

She pulls away slightly breathless and resumes her mission. Still touching over my shorts, she trails her finger along the ridges of my dick, causing it to jump at the contact while I groan, which makes her smile.

My wolf is howling at me to claim her, but I will not rush her. Everything is up to her—when she wants it, how she wants it, and currently this is what she wants.

"Can you take your shorts off for me? I can't manhandle you the way you do me."

I chuckle as I hook my thumbs into my shorts, lift my hips off the bed, and slide them down my thighs.

When my dick is free to stand at full attention, her eyes nearly double in size before she turns her face to mine.

"Th-that is supposed to fit inside me at some point?" she asks in a half laugh, half bark.

I allow myself to grip the shaft and pump it just once, nodding to her.

She smacks my hand away from myself and continues her investigation. As she leans in to reach for me, I reach around her and grab one smooth globe of her ass in my hand. Her small stature means literally her whole ass cheek fits perfectly in my palm, and it takes serious concentration not to blow my load right here and now.

When Leera's fingers begin to trace the tight skin of my shaft, the tingles and heat of the mate bond flare through me, and, *fuck,* I forgot what this felt like.

When she reaches the thicker, meaty area at the base, she looks at it with renewed intrigue before turning her attention to me.

"I've never seen a man in real life, but I know basic anatomy, and this," she says, squeezing my knot, causing me to drop my head and moan, "is not in any text books."

I'm panting when I lift my eyes back to hers. "That, Sweetheart, is my knot. Werewolves have similar anatomy to our wolf counterparts. That is a piece of me that only a mate can take into their body. It's primarily for breeding, and it's very..." I'm cut off by another groan because she's gently squeezing it again. "Uuughh, it's very sensitive."

She nods and returns to where she was examining my body. She trails her fingers under my knot to my sack and gently holds it in her hands.

Grandmas. Angry fans. Hockey plays. Sweaty gym socks. I struggle to keep my mind anywhere but here, praying I don't cum all over her face while she's trying to learn my body.

"Le-leera, baby," I breathe.

She turns to look at me.

"Also very sensitive."

She just smiles and nods before coming back up to my chest and kissing me. Hard. Her fingers are digging into my shoulders, and she moves herself so that she's once again straddling me, causing me to groan into her mouth, breaking the kiss. She nips at my lip.

"Is my little mate getting feisty?" I ask in a husky voice I barely recognize.

"The thought definitely crossed my mind," she says as she pulls away from me and takes her shirt off.

My Pucking Family

Goddess, grant me control.

23
Leera

I have no idea what I'm doing. I'm just doing what feels right here, and it seems to be working, if his reactions are anything to go by.

"What do you want me to do, baby?" he asks, chest heaving.

I travel back down to his very hard, silky-smooth dick and wrap my hand around it for the first time. His head falls back, and he groans again.

"Can you show me what to do? I want to make you feel good."

His eyes burn with desire—and maybe even something stronger—when he nods and his hand meets mine.

He slowly lifts my hand to the top of his length before slowly gliding it back down. "This is the basic motion. No matter what you do, it's going to be perfect," he says as he rubs the side of my face.

He pulls his hand away, and I try it again by myself this time. Keeping my grip, I slide my hand up the seven or eight inches of length above his knot, brushing my thumb across the tip, earning myself another moan from my mate.

I continue moving like he showed me, but I move a little quicker, and when I get to the top, I rotate my hand around the head.

Every moan, grunt, and groan spurs me on further. I feel so empowered and in control. To have this man. This famous hockey player. A seven-hundred-and-thirteen-year-old werewolf, in pleasure and at my mercy, because of me…it's a feeling that can't be explained.

How can something be as hard as steel beneath such soft skin?

His hips have started wiggling with my movements, like he's struggling to stay still. Instead of slowing down and taking it easy on him, I decide to test my limits. Thinking back to when I was lost in the heat, my most frantic moments were just before the fireworks erupted.

With his head tilted back, eyes clamped shut, mouth open, panting in the pleasure that I'm giving him, I lean forward, and when my hand moves down his shaft, I twirl my tongue around the slit of his dick.

His eyes immediately fly open, his head snapping back up, and he growls deep in his chest, watching me even more intently now.

High on the power of making him feel the way he made me feel, I continue stroking him while licking the top like a Tootsie Pop. After a few minutes of enjoying wringing pleasure from his body, he's barking my name, "Leera. Leera, baby, I'm going to…" But if he's going to come, I want all of him. I want to experience this.

I double my efforts and his hips stutter before he locks up and roars my name, just as salty spurts of him flood my mouth.

I try to swallow, but *shit, that's gross.* I spit it out as gracefully as I can.

"Holy hell," is all he says as he pulls me back up onto the bed, lying me beside him. I notice his cock is still pulsing, like I kept pulsing.

I wonder if he'll want to go again, like I did.

"Did I…did I do okay?" I ask, feeling my insecurities trying to rise again.

"Di-wh-are," he tries to speak. He shakes his head and tries again. "Are you serious?" he asks, still trying to catch his breath.

I just nod, feeling the blush rise to my cheeks.

He pulls me back into the straddling position and kisses me, even with him still lingering in my mouth.

He pulls away to rest his forehead against mine, and I rest my hands on his still-heaving chest.

"Leera, that was incredible and more than I expected. I thought you said you'd never even seen one?" he laughs.

"I haven't; after you showed me, I just watched your reactions and trusted my instincts."

"Your instincts are fucking phenomenal," he pants out, causing me to release a breathy laugh.

"Sorry I spit it out, but the texture is…" and I trial off in another small gag. *How do women do that?*

He throws his head back and laughs. The sound of his laughter vibrating through my body as I rest against his chest has me really hoping he wants to go again.

24
ROMAN

Everything about my existence has gone from the mundane day-to-day of checking on my pack, playing hockey, and spending time with only my trusted men to a whirlwind of everything I never expected. There's no way I could have seen any of this coming, and I wouldn't have it any other way.

Leera's heat seemed to unlock the need brought on by the mate bond. It's getting harder and harder not to take her when we're together, and I know she's feeling it too because she's been a horny little thing. I'm not saying I mind that she wants me, but I know I need to give her time to accept that her life is changing unexpectedly, and I'm realizing it is more difficult than I thought it would be to hold out this long. All of that with the addition of consistently reminding myself that she's a virgin, and I want to make sure she's completely ready. I want it to be an experience for her. In my continued research of human relationships, women will remember this day forever in a different way than men, and well, werewolves too.

Though werewolves definitely seem to take it more seriously

than human men, it's still so much different than women. All of which leads me to wonder if werewolf traditions that are so based on instinct make us take some things for granted.

When the time comes and she's ready, I know I want to make it everything she's ever dreamed of.

In addition to balancing Leera's need, we're also learning to balance our lives. She's been staying in my room, but she has requested her own room for when Zoey stays the night and for if she feels like she needs space.

Again, I find myself questioning my instincts and wondering if maybe instincts alone aren't enough, because I immediately want to say no. She's staying with me; Zoey can have a room that they can decorate however they want. However, I already know how well that would go over with my independent little mate. While it makes my hackles rise at the thought of her wanting her own space away from me, I have to remember to think about her needs from her perspective and not our archaic notions.

She's currently in *our* room, packing her bags for her first away game, which is a victory in itself. I truly thought she would have fought harder about the away game situation, but I should have known she always has a plan. She got in touch with Sinclair and planned an assignment on the lives of hockey players on the road. I had asked her if she wanted to be part of any of the press briefings, but she declined after everything that's happened.

I'm sitting in my office, pretending to be busy doing something because I know she's adjusting to me being around all the time, and I don't want to smother her until she's ready. I've already arranged our visit to the pack in a couple of days for what we think will be Leera's first transition into her wolf. I can feel the pack beaming with excitement at the thought of meeting their future Luna through our bonds.

The men are all coming with us as well. They claim it's for Leera's protection, but I can feel their excitement, just like everyone else's. We haven't all been to the pack for a full moon in far too long, and I make a note to discuss making a schedule to be there for my pack more often on special occasions.

With nothing else to do at the moment, I decide to clean up my desk. Just as I start shuffling a few pages around, Matilda slowly swings the door open. "Here he is, Dearie," she says in her sweet, old voice as she reveals Leera fidgeting behind her.

In an instant, she's turned back to me, scowling and pointing her wrinkled finger at me. "Roman Razboinic, maybe make sure your mate knows where your office is if you're going to hole yourself up in here. She couldn't find you."

Shit. I'm on my feet and moving towards the door, feeling Leera's anxiety rolling off her.

"Thank you, Miss Tilly," she squeaks as Matilda hugs her, glaring and pointing at me once more for good measure.

"You're welcome. All is well. You keep this lughead in line for me, will ya?" She baits Leera into a sniffly giggle.

I pull Leera to me and watch as Matilda shuffles away. "I'm so fucking sorry, Sweetheart. I was trying to give you space. I was worried I would overwhelm you, and I still fucked up."

"It's…I'm okay. I don't know why I get so worked up. I tried to call you, but your phone was in the kitchen, and my mind just kind of spiraled a little." She shakes her head as she finishes, like she's trying to dislodge the anxious parts of her mind.

I hug her body close to mine, tipping her chin up with my finger. "I'm here. I'll be more aware of my cell phone so that you can contact me until you're able to reach me through our bond."

I can see the wheels turning in her head before she asks, "We haven't talked about it directly, but you can, what, like hear each other's thoughts?"

"Not exactly, but kind of. Packs have the ability to communicate telepathically. Once we seal our mate bond, you'll be part of the pack, and you'll be able to speak directly to us."

"And to…to complete our mate bond, we have to…we have to…you know?" she stutters, suddenly shy again.

This won't do.

Her anxiety is still weighing on her, so I close the door and pull her farther into my office. I lift her up and set her on top of my desk as I take my seat in front of her, sliding my hands up the insides of her thighs.

"Wh-what are you doing?"

"Shhh. Relax. I'm ridding you of your anxious thoughts that I caused," I purr. "And yes, to solidify our mate bond, we will have sex, and while my knot is inside of you, we will bite each other here." I kiss and nibble at the tender skin at the base of her neck, causing goosebumps to break out down her arms. "You'll feel our bond effectively snapping into place. We'll be able to speak to each other without saying a word. We'll be able to feel each other's emotions much more strongly."

As I explain everything, I continue to touch her. Tease her. Taste her between words.

When I finish my explanation, I look into her eyes, smiling to myself, when I see that the desire has chased the fear away.

"Feel better?" I ask, still allowing my fingers to roam across her body.

She nods before asking only one word: "When?"

I smile at her, hoping she can see how much she means to

me as I lift her hand to my lips, leaving a long kiss on her knuckles. "When you tell me that you're ready, without a doubt or worry in your mind."

"Thank you, Roman." She leans forward, kissing me hard. "I think…" she trails off, and for a moment I take her kisses and wait for her to find her words.

She grabs hold of my shoulders and hops off of the edge of the desk into my lap, and I catch her, molding our bodies together.

She stops kissing me and wraps both her arms around me, hiding her face in my neck where I nibble hers. She takes a deep breath of my scent, so I do the same, just soaking her in when she whispers, "I think I'm falling for you, Roman."

My heart stops. Then it soars. She holds me tighter, like she's hiding from embarrassment for having admitted what she's feeling. Needing to see her gorgeous icy-blue eyes, I slowly pull her arms from around my neck, and as I hold her head in my hands, I kiss the tip of her nose.

I look into her eyes, speaking to her, her wolf, her soul, "Hear me now when I say that I already know I love you. I love you, Leera Adams. I love your strength. I love your kindness. I love the way you make this townhouse feel like home for the first time since it was built. I love how you light up every room you enter, no matter where we go, and you don't even know it. I love watching you watch your favorite movies. I love the look on your face when you take your first sip of coffee of the day. I love the way your body fits perfectly with mine. Even if you weren't my second chance at having my soul mate. Even if you were just the human girl you thought you were when we met. Even though I've loved your soul before. I know now that it's not just the bond. It's you, Leera. I. Love. You."

Her eyes fill with tears at my sudden need to make her understand that this is more than just the mate bond. I've done this her way—the human way. I've learned so much about her in a way werewolves normally miss out on at first. Instead of diving into the mate bond and solidifying it immediately and throwing ourselves into a life together, it's allowed me to know her at a level I never knew I needed.

She tries to find words, but her emotions are running too high. I crash my lips to hers and let our tangling tongues convey everything left unsaid.

Our kiss takes a frenzied turn, and she's sliding her hands under my shirt, lightly running her nails down my chest. I groan into her mouth as my dick hardens beneath her. She begins to wriggle in my lap, whimpering into the kiss. With one hand holding her tighter to my lap and the other reaching under her hoodie in search of her nipple, she arches into me when there's a knock at my office door.

Before I can growl at Benny to go away, the door is swinging open, and the smile on his face says he's immensely proud of himself. "Everyone packed and ready? We've gotta leave in thirty minutes to hop on the plane for tomorrow's game."

Leera scrambles off my lap, blushing from embarrassment now instead of the heat collecting in her tiny purple thong she put on this morning, and I do growl this time, my boner now on display for everyone in the room to see.

Benny's just leans against the door frame with his arms crossed, still smiling like I'm not going to pummel him for this later, when the twins walk past my office door.

Only they don't keep walking. I hear them stop and then

see them step backwards back into the doorway, now wearing ornery smiles to match Benny's.

I will kill you all if you don't stop embarrassing her and leave now.

"Keep the old man in line for us, will ya, Leera?" Benny jests as he ushers the twins away, pulling the door closed behind them.

"Fuck, I'm sorry…" I begin when Leera suddenly bursts out laughing.

When she gets it all out of her system, she starts wiping tears from her eyes.

"Whew. I can't believe they just caught us like that. I'm sorry, but it was just like a scene out of a movie, and I couldn't help but laugh."

My face must portray my confusion because she uses her thumbs to smooth the wrinkle between my brows before planting a kiss there.

"Come on, Big Guy, we've got a plane to catch."

25
Leera

I've been on airplanes.

I've flown all over the world.

I've flown in economy, business class, and first class.

I have never flown on a private jet.

I have never been on a plane crammed full of hockey-playing werewolves.

As we climb the stairs into the team's private jet with their massive logo covering the entire side, I realize I'm nervous, and it takes me a moment to sift through my thoughts to figure out why.

I know I'm safe.

I know I'll be with Roman.

I know all of the guys that I know will be here.

But what if the others don't like me?

The rest of the men on the team aren't pack members, they're just teammates. They don't have a loyalty to Roman outside of hockey.

We pass through the doorway of the plane, and Coach is

standing there with his clipboard marking off his men as they climb inside. "Well, hello there, young lady. It's nice to see you again," he greets me with a giant smile, immediately calming some of my worry.

"Hey, Coach." I smile back, hoping he can't see the nervousness on my face.

He claps me on the shoulder before turning to Roman. "You take care of her now, Roman. She's a treasure." And with that, I really smile.

Roman, being the grump he is, just nods and grunts at Coach like a caveman.

My eyes roll so hard, I worry they'll get stuck like that.

Coach laughs. "She'll fit in just fine."

Roman leads me to our seats. I gawk in awe of everything. Who needs business or first class when you can fly like this? The seats are basically couches with seatbelts in them. There are giant TV screens everywhere with different hockey games playing on them. There are even a couple of miniature refrigerators nestled in between the seats.

When Roman takes his seat, instead of letting me plop into mine, he pulls me onto his lap in front of EVERYONE. I've got to be bright red. "Roman, would you like to clue me in on why I can't sit in my own seat?" I whisper harshly in his ear.

Benny chuckles from beside us, reminding me whispering probably doesn't work well on an airplane full of werewolves.

Shit.

Roman just chuckles to himself before responding, "Sorry, Sweetheart, but we're on an airplane full of unmated werewolves, and you smell like heaven. It's not your fault, and it's not theirs either. So, I'm just going to hang on to you, if you're comfortable, that is?"

Of course he would end it with a question and give me an out if I really wanted it. Turns out, I don't. I've still got to get used to all the public displays of affection, but I love them. They catch me off guard because I'm not used to it, but that doesn't mean I don't enjoy his possessiveness.

As the men continue to file onto the plane, I settle into Roman's lap with my laptop to finish one of my assignments.

In the last few days, I've also realized I don't hate taking my college classes online. I actually really enjoy it. It's a lot more like homeschooling. I get to work at my own pace and don't have to deal with the disruptions that come with the classroom environment. I've actually worked ahead in my Explorations in Modern Mathematics class and only have five assignments left to complete for the entire semester. I've always loved math; something about it just clicks in my brain, so for that class especially, being able to work ahead at my own pace is really nice.

Benny is sitting on Roman's left, Andrei is sitting on his right, the twins are giving Coach hell, and Slate is tucked away in a corner with his own laptop.

Benny keeps asking me questions about my classes and being his normal sunshiny self while Roman grunts along. He's got everyone else fooled with his tough guy attitude, but I'm learning it's because if he lets too many people in, then he has more people that he'll care about and worry over.

With Andrei on his right, my back is facing him, and I can't help but get that feeling I always get every time Andrei is around. I don't know why I haven't told Roman about the bond-like tugging feeling I also get from him. I think we mostly haven't really had a quiet moment for me to really bring it up. I should have when we were talking through everything the other day, but our list was already so long. I can feel the tiny tugging feeling now, and it's going to drive me crazy.

I want to bring it up, talk to him—something—but a crowded plane of nosey werewolves isn't the place, so I just keep working through my remaining math assignments and occasionally answering Benny's questions, until Roman tenses beneath me.

When I look up at him, he's staring straight at Slate, and they're definitely having a silent conversation that the six of them are all in on because they all go from staring at Slate to Roman, or me, I'm not sure.

"What's up?" I whisper to Roman, but he shakes his head and gives me a look that I think says, *I'll explain later.*

26
ROMAN

I've got it. I've got it all, Slate confirms.

Explain, I demand.

I've got extensive communication trails between India and both of your fathers. I've also finally linked your father to that subdivision that was being built that we found Leera in, and the likely paper trail from him paying those rogues to kidnap her, he elaborates.

My blood is boiling, and I know she can feel the tension coursing through my body. Judging by the look of everyone, I think most of the plane can feel it.

The only thing I can't find or confirm is why, Slate finishes.

I sit and think for a minute before I believe with certainty that, *If my father kidnapped and drugged Leera because she was "in his way," it's safe to assume...* I trail off; *it's safe to assume my father is likely the one responsible for Imogen and my child's murder.*

Each of my men just nod their heads.

We need to find out why, and why his scent was nowhere to be found either time. Leera said she heard a snobby rich guy bossing the lackey around; we know that had to be him checking on things himself, but he left no trace of a scent, Benny interjects.

It has to be part of why India and I were arranged to wed and become king and queen, I think out loud between my men and myself.

Slate nods again and dives back into his laptop.

I know that Slate will do everything in his power to find any and all the information we need. I thought it would feel different to get confirmation of what a monster my father is. I thought I'd be more hurt. Maybe more angry? I am all of those things, but the level of intensity in those feelings isn't as debilitating as I anticipated they would be.

I can only assume it's the result of the perfect little silver-haired miracle sitting on my lap.

She's typing away on her laptop, working on her schoolwork. I think she's enjoying the online classes more than she expected but doesn't want to admit it out loud.

Every now and then she grabs her notebook to work out a math problem then hops right back to her laptop; I wish I could be in her mind, watching how it works.

My mate is smart. She's flying through mathematics that I could never understand. I'm not a numbers kind of guy. I'm a history and military strategy kind of guy.

How would I feel right now if I learned all this without Leera in my life? Or even right before I found her?

I would be at risk of turning feral, I have no doubt. It's rare, but it's possible. If someone becomes so lost in anger, their wolf can take over control of their bodies, and sometimes they never give it back. Luckily, it's about as rare as second-chance mates.

We'll get Leera all caught up on everything we've learned as soon as I get to show her a few surprises we put together for her.

Just the thought of the happiness on her face forces a wide smile on my own.

The smile only lasts a moment, though; it fades once I remember that my mate was kidnapped. She was kidnapped and drugged and might have been murdered had we not arrived in time. And it was all orchestrated by my father. My own flesh and fucking blood.

What could be so fucking important that he would take my mate from me? Again?

Nothing. That's all there is to it. There is nothing in this world or any other world worth the life of my mate.

Now we have to find out why. We have to figure out how to stop him. We have to figure out how he's masking his scent.

All the thoughts crashing around my brain bring my wolf just under my skin. He wants to growl, but I can feel that he knows it will put Leera even further on edge.

27
Leera

By the time the plane lands, there is palpable tension in the air. All of the six men who I know have been so on edge the entire flight that it made it hard to concentrate. Not knowing what is causing this kind of tension is even more frustrating; I want to know what they aren't telling me.

While the rest of the men are visibly amped up for the game, the starting six look like they'd rather go to war. With the majority of the team whooping and hollering, the seven of us descend the steps of the plane in terse silence. I want to push them to tell me what's going on, but again, I know it's not the time or place.

Luckily, we've arrived the day before the game and have a couple hours before the team wants to get some ice time in later this evening.

The ride to the hotel is, again, silent to the point that I'm becoming uncomfortable. I spend that time sitting in the front seat while Roman drives, trying to keep my anxiety from rising.

What if it has to do with me?

Did I do something wrong?

Why won't they tell me what's going on?

I can feel the swirl of panic slowly taking up all the space inside my body. Just as I feel the threatening burn of tears, I'm only vaguely aware of Roman leaving the vehicle.

Weren't we driving down the road?

I try to focus on my surroundings, but all I can hear is the angry pounding of my blood. My surroundings are now a blur from the water collecting in my eyes.

All of a sudden, I'm being pulled from the car, lightning zapping up my arm, and then I'm wrapped in a solid embrace.

Roman, my soul seems to whisper.

"I'm so fucking sorry, Leera," he says into my hair.

"W-wait, why are you s-sorry?" I whisper, trying to sound strong, but it comes out all nasally.

"Leera, baby, you're having a panic attack. What do you mean, why am I sorry? This is my fault. Fuck! Are you okay?"

I continue to just stare at him, my brain refusing to connect the dots; instead, all any part of my body can focus on is him.

"I didn't mean to not talk to you about this; I was waiting until we got somewhere that it felt safe for us to discuss what came up," he continues.

All I can do is nod my head while the haze of the anxiety is slowly chased away by the cherry and leather protection of my mate.

He continues kissing the top of my head as he rubs circles on my back.

When I've finally calmed down, I realize we're literally sitting on the side of the road, the SUV idling next to us with the other five of our group.

"I-I'm sorry. I didn't even notice it setting in until it was too late. I knew something bothered you guys on the plane. I was trying to patiently wait for information, but my mind started spinning."

"Shhh, you never have to apologize to me for this. I've got you." He takes a deep breath. "I'm the one that's sorry. Things like this will be easier once we're mated and you can be in on our conversations," he finishes with an ornery smirk on his handsome face.

"Come on, let's go; anyone could see us sitting out here. I'm okay." I smile and pull on his hand, like I'm actually capable of helping him get up off the ground. "Let's go to the hotel and get settled, and then you can tell me everything at once."

Roman just smiles and nods and helps me back into the car.

When we finally arrive at the hotel, it's freaking gorgeous. In my travels with my parents, we stayed in a lot of different locations, but they weren't the lavish ones. They were comfortable and homey feeling. This screams money that I cannot even fathom. For a moment, I'm plagued by thoughts of whether or not I'm good enough.

That moment is abruptly cut off by Benny.

"Do you like it, Leera? Roman wanted somewhere nice for you to stay on your first away game experience. We usually stay somewhere more basic, but someone"—he shoots Roman one of his sunshine smiles—"requested an upgrade from our usual quarters."

My jaw drops, and I immediately whirl around to face Roman. "You did this for me? Roman, you know that doesn't matter to me!"

He takes my hands in his, brings them to his mouth, and kisses them, then says, "The fact that you don't is part of why I love you. I wanted to do something special for you. I knew it would be a nice surprise."

I fly forward and kiss him in front of everyone, right in the middle of this gorgeous hotel lobby under a twinkling chandelier.

After kissing him senseless for this obnoxiously sweet surprise, but hearing him say those words, I remember that we're in a very public place when someone whoops from somewhere near us.

Embarrassment courses through my veins when I pull away to find a small crowd has gathered and is just sitting there watching us.

Oh, no, did they take pictures?
Will that upset Roman?

Andrei comes forward as Roman pulls me back into his body, smiling like a fool. "Alright, everyone, move along, beat it!" Andrei hollers as he approaches us with the hotel keys to our room.

I mouth a silent *thank you* to him before letting Roman whisk me away to the elevators. Only, we're not alone. All five of his men pile into the elevator with us, causing me to smother a giggle at all these men crammed into such a small space.

I notice the elevator just keeps climbing when we finally reach the top and it stops. Roman scans our room key on a pad within the elevator that I didn't notice was there.

That seems backward; aren't the card pads usually just outside the door to the rooms?

The elevator dings and the doors part, revealing a massive sparkling room with a giant circular cream-colored couch right in the middle. The whole space is circular and then branches off like one of those highway roundabouts.

"Is this like an upstairs lobby or something?" I ask with a huffed laugh as I tentatively step inside.

Roman's hand on my lower back increases pressure, pushing me farther into the space. "No, Sweetheart, this is the presidential suite of the hotel. Each of those"—he moves his arms, pointing to the branching doorways I noticed—"leads to each bedroom. You can pick ours, and the guys can squabble over what's left."

"Will I ever get used to this?" I mean to say to myself as I stare at the space in total awe that this is my life now.

"Whether or not you do, it will still be real. I still have to convince myself every day that you're really here," he says as he tucks a strand of hair behind my ears.

What the hell am I supposed to say to that?

He's always had a way with words, but it seems as of late, those words knock on my heart and race straight for my lower abdomen. I still melt into a gooey puddle of the sweet things he says and all, but now it also leaves puddles in my panties, and I can't seem to get enough of him. *Is that what the L word is like, or is it just the mate bond?* I'll have to ask Zoey.

I turn to him and smile before pulling away and venturing through the doorways to pick a room.

The men are all lounging on what used to look like a giant couch, but with all of them on it, it's kind of lost its grandeur. I've got one more room to look at before making my choice when there's a ding noise coming from the elevator doors.

I shit you not, all six of them turn their heads and growl. I think one of them barked, and I can't help the snort that escapes me at the scene, which I immediately try to hide with a cough. They really are just a bunch of overgrown lap dogs.

Slate makes his way to the doors and checks a small digital screen to the right. "Looks like it's for you, Roman," he begins. When he notices my change in body language, he quickly adds, "It's not her," and I wish it didn't instantly remove the weight on my shoulders.

When Roman opens the door, it's not someone I'd expect that comes through.

28
ROMAN

With all the information that Slate was finally able to uncover, I forgot the other part of Leera's surprise. I meant to talk to her about this one, so she wouldn't be blindsided, but it's too late now. I didn't even remember to give my men a heads-up.

Khaos walks into the room like he owns the place as I follow in behind him.

"Men, you know Khaos; and Leera, I believe you've met," I begin, trying to break the ice, but it falls flat. Leera's crossed her arms across her chest in what she thinks is an intimidating pose, when really, she's just pushing her perfect little breasts up higher in the air.

"Care to share with the class, Boss," Benny grunts.

"Not entirely; Khaos, Leera, and I need to have a conversation. Once that's over with, we'll fill the rest of you in."

I'm met with bewildered stares when I add to my men, *It's Leera's business to share with you, not mine.*

It didn't help with the confusion on their faces, but it's lessening the feeling that I left them out of something.

"Shall we?" I ask, directing Leera and Khaos towards the glass doors of the patio.

Leera just nods, arms still wrapped around her chest, and heads towards the door.

Khaos can't help but ruffle feathers and says, "It's okay, boys; we won't be long," as he waltzes towards the balcony.

I scrub my hand down my face, wondering if I made the right choice. *I'll let you know if I decide I'd rather toss him off the building.*

That gets me a few chuckles and some additional tension releases from my men, so I move to join the others overlooking the city.

As I step through the patio's glass door, I find Leera quietly fidgeting to my right and Khaos to my left trying to maintain his difficult, indifferent mask, but Leera's presence is clearly affecting him. I wish I had remembered to give Leera the heads up. Khaos, on the other hand, has no idea what's happening and came because I did something I thought I'd never do—I asked him for help.

Closing the door behind me, I turn to Leera. "I hope you don't mind that I asked Khaos to join us for the away game. I meant to tell you so it was a smaller surprise than him just showing up."

She offers me a tentative smile and nods her head.

"Would you like to tell him, or should I?" I ask her, as a smile I can't control takes over my whole face, causing her to smile as well.

She takes the two steps to reach me, wraps her arms around me, and tips her head back to look me in the eyes. "You can tell him. You two have more history than we do."

I lean down to kiss her forehead. As I lift my head, I can clearly read the confusion radiating from Khaos.

"Do you feel the bond between the two of you?" I ask him.

His eyebrows come together as he slowly turns his head to look at me, not able to ignore the situation any longer.

"Leera is my mate," I state plainly and allow him time to absorb what I've just said.

His initial reaction is anger; I can see it taking over his features now. He can feel the bond, but, like me, he hasn't allowed himself to accept what he believes isn't possible.

"That isn't possible," he growls.

"Tell me you don't feel it," I say clearly and calmly, pulling Leera's body to rest against the front of mine.

He shakes his head and growls again as he turns to grip the railing of the balcony.

"I know how you're feeling," I begin. "I know you think it's not possible, so you think it might be easier to just ignore it. You think maybe you've been cursed or that it's all in your head, but ask your wolf. Our souls know more than we ever will."

After a moment, I watch as he slowly relaxes and must be accepting the information we've presented him with.

"How is this possible?" His voice can barely be heard with the wind raging around us, but I hear him, and so does my little miracle.

She looks up to me before she pats my arm and pulls away, walking towards where he's standing.

"Hey?" she says, almost making it sound like a question. "Can we sit and talk? It's a lot of information, and when I'm done you can ask me any questions you have."

He nods and follows her to the patio furniture, where we all take a seat. She starts with her childhood, knowing nothing of werewolves, losing her parents earlier this year, adjusting to college, and then the day we met.

The cool and collected Khaos looks exactly how I felt the day she walked into my life. To be fair, because it's so rare, so few know this is even possible.

She continues explaining that she felt the bond between them and everything we've gone through since, including her kidnapping and India's anger towards her.

The last bit set mine and his blood to boil by the tension in the air, but not enough that it affected Leera.

"And so, if we're not mistaken, you were my soul's brother in a previous life, and we wanted you to know. We don't have to have any specific kind of relationship if you don't want or anything; we—I—just wanted to make sure you knew," she finishes with an uneasy smile on her face and her head tilting slightly to the right. Her fingers are a little shaky, but she keeps herself together well. I wish I could tell her I am proud of her, using our bond. *Soon.*

Khaos is scrubbing his hands through his hair, almost as if he's hoping the answers will materialize there and land on the table in front of him.

I use this moment to let him know how much I truly need him in this situation. "The reason I asked you here specifically, instead of having you come to our home, is that I need your help."

I again wait to allow him all the time he needs to absorb and understand what I'm saying.

His hands fall into his lap as he leans back in his chair.

"What is it?"

"With Leera being kidnapped and us still not knowing the extent of the situation," I'm not ready to tell him *everything*. "I need to know she's okay when I, or one of my men, can't be there. I know you have your own life and hockey games, but I'm hoping that you can sit with Leera at the game so that she's not alone and so that she's safe."

"Why me and not one of your guards?" It sounds like he replied automatically without allowing himself to accept what we've told him, and I notice Leera flinches the tiniest amount at his tone.

"Shit, I'm sorry. I'm not good with feelings, Leera. I didn't mean that against you," he quickly adds, also noticing her reaction.

"To answer your question, as much as I trust my pack guards, they're not prepared for whatever's going on here. I need to know she's safe, and I knew once we told you about the bond, you'd be just as protective of her as I am, or at least that was my hope."

He allows himself a moment to think. I reach over and take Leera's hand in mine, pulling her out of her seat and into my lap so I can hold her.

"How did you know? How did you accept it?" he asks, and I can feel the anguish he still feels over Imogen.

"I didn't. Even with my wolf raging in my mind that she was our mate, I didn't allow myself to believe it because it couldn't be true." I pull Leera even tighter to me. "Until my elder came and told me that it has happened in history, but only a few times. She said witches cannot recreate any of our sacred bonds, and that at the end of the day, our wolf knows."

He nods again, and for a few minutes, I think that's all the reply that he'll give us.

"And after everything, you didn't keep her from me?" he asks me with an ancient pain in his voice that I know all too well.

"It was never my goal to keep her from you. We just wanted to build our life together, and you didn't want that for us. We both lost her five hundred years ago..." I allow myself a moment to rein my emotions back in. "And we both deserve this second chance with her now."

Leera's small hand cups the side of my face and pulls me until my eyes meet hers, then brings my forehead to hers for a moment as if she's trying to speak to me too.

"I may not be the one you lost, but I'm here now. I may not know my wolf yet, but I will. I just want us all to be happy and safe." Her sweet voice and kind touch anchor me in the moment.

Khaos looks to Leera and says, "I'd like to join you for the game, if you'll have my company?"

"Yes!" she squeals. "Though this kind and charming thing is kind of weirding me out. I think I like cocky and obnoxious Khaos better," she jokes, causing us all to laugh.

When was the last time we laughed together, Khaos and I?

As if he heard me, we lock eyes for a moment before it's broken by the sound of Leera's stomach growling. We both snap our heads in her direction.

"What? Serious conversations make me hungry."

And we're laughing again, and I stand from my seat, bringing Leera with me. I lift her up and allow myself to nuzzle her neck before setting her back on her feet.

"What would you like to eat, Sweetheart? I don't think there's anything they don't have here in Dover."

"Oh gosh. You know I can never decide. Can't you let the

guys pick? As long as it's not spicy, I'll be fine," she retorts.

"I know just the place," Khaos announces.

While Leera gets ready to go eat dinner with all of us but Slate—who wants to hang back and make sure he's not missing anything—Khaos and I catch my men up on the conversation we had outside, after getting Leera's permission to tell them.

Benny had already picked up on the situation. Andrei looked frustrated. The twins are still adamant they don't want to go all mushy for a mate of their own. And Slate was, well, Slate. At least now they all know.

The next step will be sitting down and discussing everything that he found with Leera and maybe Khaos too. If he's going to help keep her safe, he needs to know what's going on.

29
Leera

Dinner was wonderfully uncomfortable.

It was wonderful in the fact that the food was beyond delicious, and we basically had our first giant family dinner.

The uncomfortable parts were just the men being all together with Khaos, I think. The energy was a bit off. They weren't as loose. It's hard to explain, but it's like each one of them were waiting for the other to do something to piss them off. Roman and I kept trying to lighten the mood when we could, but you can't undo hundreds of years of animosity in one evening.

Add "Group Bonding" to my ever-growing list of things to tackle.

Since Khaos wanted to choose the restaurant, he led us to the absolute cutest seafood restaurant that's actually on a boating dock with outside seating overlooking the water. It was too chilly to sit outside, but I made a mental note to come back when it's warm and enjoy the view.

The food was beyond incredible. It had been a while since I had some really fresh fish and shrimp. We made it through mostly unscathed, and when we finished up, we all headed back to the hotel where the men left Khaos and me while they went to warm up for the game tomorrow.

I kiss Roman goodbye and plop down on the couch, patting my very full stomach and releasing a heavy sigh.

"Penny for your thoughts?" Khaos asks as he lowers himself onto the other side of the couch.

"Ha! Where do I even start? I mean, you got the rundown earlier; I'm still just trying to process everything myself."

He nods, and I think we're just going to sit here quietly when he says, "I don't know why Roman and I were given another chance with you, but you must be very important to the Moon Goddess..." He looks up to me, and there is more emotion than I've ever seen swirling in those smokey-gray eyes. "But I promise to be a better brother this time."

His voice cracks on the last word, and so does my heart. I lean forward, resting my elbows on the tops of my legs and admit, "Hey, I don't have any memories from before. I don't know if I ever will, but I can tell you my soul—my wolf—she doesn't hold any animosity towards you. I feel no negative energies from her at all."

He lifts his chin to look at me and says, "Really?"

Lifting the left side of my lips into a half smile, I reply, "Really. I wish they could talk to us so we didn't have to guess everything, but it almost feels like she wants to...being a werewolf is so weird...she wants to like brush against you? She and I are still trying to understand each other after her being poisoned for so long, so I hope I got that right."

He releases a tired chuckle, but it also looks like some of the tension drains from his body.

"Do you mind if I get a little more schoolwork done while the guys are gone?"

"Not at all. I'm still trying to process everything myself." With that, he finally allows himself to really relax and turns on the sports channel to watch the hockey updates while I scurry to my room and back with my laptop in tow.

We spend the rest of the evening in quiet comfort. Him flipping through the channels, me working on my lessons. Even when the men get back from warm-ups, everyone just kind of blends together.

I'd be a big fat liar if I said I didn't really enjoy getting into these amicable places like a real family.

30
KHAOS

I can't believe this is happening.

Even with her sitting right in front of me.

Even being able to feel the family bond tethered to my soul.

Even with my wolf's confirmation.

It still doesn't feel real.

I wouldn't allow myself to believe what the tugging could be when I met her at their game that night.

I still wouldn't be able to if Roman hadn't clearly explained everything he went through. It's a shock to get my baby sister back, in a way. I can't even fathom what it would feel like to be one of the very few selected by the Moon Goddess to have their soul mate returned to them within the same life cycle.

But that also means Leera is important. It could be Roman, but I'm not giving him that kind of credit yet. It has to be her. She's always been so bright and pure. The world needs more souls like hers.

It's weird being here with Roman and his men, though. Since we started playing hockey, there hasn't been a game where we crossed paths that wasn't an all-out war.

Now, we're all sitting here pretending we haven't spent over five hundred years hating each other.

How long will we be able to pretend? Are we capable of forming an acquaintance-ship at the least, or a friendship at most? Maybe we'll have to settle on medium ground and just be allies.

I guess we're going to find out, because I'm not abandoning her again. I fucked up last time. I let my hatred towards Roman keep me from the only person I've ever loved. My little sister was the only person in any of the worlds who ever meant anything to me.

I blame Roman for her death, but he doesn't know that I blame myself just as much.

31
ROMAN

This is the first time that I haven't met up with Leera at the game. I'm getting to see her whole process of getting ready for the game. She lays all her clothes out on the bed before she goes to take a shower and whatever-the-fuck women spend forever doing in the bathroom.

She's trying to kill me. She has to be. She laid out satin black panties, with a matching bra. Then she's got those skintight pants that look like black leather. For her tops, she has a black t-shirt, a black hoodie, and the jersey that I got her.

She comes out with just a towel on, and what little bit of motivation I may have had to put myself together has been obliterated.

"Will I be able to get dressed with you in the room, or should I take my clothes into the bathroom?" she scolds lovingly with her hands on her hips as she smiles.

I rise from where I am sitting and slowly walk towards her, watching as the blush begins to spread. Just as it hits the tip of her nose, the scent of her arousal reaches me.

Dragging a finger across her exposed collarbone, I growl, "Why don't you let me help?"

I flick the towel, and it falls to the ground, leaving my perfect little mate standing bare before me.

"I should make sure you're good and relaxed before the game, so you can truly enjoy it," I say softly as I lean in to take a lungful of her scent.

"H-how would you do that?" she asks as her chest begins to rise and fall more quickly.

Fuck, I love this woman.

"Well, first, I would walk you over to the wall for support," I explain before kissing her behind the ear and slowly moving her towards the wall.

She nods and nearly whimpers.

"Then I would sink to my knees to *worship* you."

Her eyes widen with lust and surprise as I lower myself to the floor and gently take one of her legs and place it on my shoulder.

"Roman," she breathes, already panting with need.

"Yes, Sunshine?"

"W-we don't have t-time for this," she stutters.

"This isn't about me. This is about you. I don't need to relax, I need to get the blood flowing. This will be the best pre-game warm up I've ever had."

Instead of another response, she gasps as I run my fingers up the inside of her thigh moving higher towards her sweet, wet center.

The scent of her alone causes my eyes to roll back in my head as I growl.

I tease her clit with my finger for a moment, and her head

falls back against the wall. When I pull my finger away from her, a whimper escapes, and she looks at me as though I've betrayed her.

"Oh, Sweetheart, I'm not done with you. We're just getting started." I smile as I lean into her body.

This time I kiss my way up the inside of her thigh, and when I reach the top, I say, "Look at me, baby; I want to watch the pleasure consume you." And with that, I close the final distance between my mouth and her sweet pussy, and her eyes enlarge even farther.

My cock is already straining against my shorts, but the moment my tongue touches her core, I'm a millisecond from blowing my load. She mewls as my tongue works her sensitive skin. Her knees become weak, and I worry that she'll fall. Without breaking contact from pleasuring my treasure, I slide her other thigh over my shoulder, place both of my hands on her lower back, and rise to my feet. She squeals, then moans as I walk her over to the bed.

I slowly lower her onto the plush bedding, and she grips my hair to hang on. I can feel the cum leaking out of my dick. If she does that again, it'll be over for me.

As soon as I lay her down and she wriggles into the bedding to get comfortable, I amp up the intensity by slowly sliding one finger into her tight pussy while I continue to devour her clit.

She somehow simultaneously melts into my touch while her body begins to coil tighter.

"Oh m-my god...Roman!" she cries as her climax consumes her. Her body clenching around my finger, spilling onto my tongue, and that does me in as I follow her over the cliff.

I lift myself from between her legs and roll over onto my

side next to her. "Are you okay?" I ask as I brush her damp hair from her face.

"Are you kidding me? I'm still floating somewhere in the stratosphere." She sighs and giggles.

Taking her hand in mine and kissing her knuckles, I say, "Then my job here is done."

She swats at me and giggles again. I rise from the bed and go to the bathroom to get her a warm rag to clean up, so she can finish getting ready.

I retake my seat in the corner of the room, just watching her in awe of her existence. Once she's gotten all her layers and make-up on, she arranges her hair into one of those messy disasters on top of her head, then adds that weird maroon glitter hair gel she bought to wear to games.

She comes out of the bathroom yet again, and her eyebrows scrunch together for a moment before she asks, "Aren't you gonna get ready?"

"Of course, Sunshine, give me ten minutes."

I lean in to kiss her on the forehead on my way to the bathroom. I took a shower this morning before Leera woke, so I just need to throw some water and a little gel in my hair and put on the suit I brought with me for game day.

The pants are black straight legs and stop just at the ankle. I add a plain white button up, leaving the top couple of buttons undone, with a black, two-button jacket over the top. Then I finish off the look with some white Alexander McQueen low-top sneakers.

When we get to the arena and I have to leave Leera with Khaos, it's a strange feeling. To trust the man who hates me with the thing I love the most in this world.

She's got her normal seat right behind our bench so that I can keep her close. When the pregame show begins, I decide that our little show at the last one made me a better hockey player. When my name is called over the loudspeakers, instead of making my lap around the ice, I go straight to my little miracle and place one hand against the glass and the other against my heart.

The smile on her face warms my once empty soul, and when I turn to Khaos, expecting a snarl or an eye roll, he's looking at her with a similar adoration. I may have been without my mate, but I think his little sister meant more to him than I ever truly understood.

32
Leera

As if I hadn't even just had a mind-blowing orgasm only a few hours ago, watching Roman play hockey turns me on more and more every time I see it.

I'm enjoying sitting here chatting it up with Khaos, but we also have absolutely no privacy right now. Social media is going to have a field day with this. Honestly, I would if it wasn't revolving around me.

Hey, that's it!

Maybe I can do a piece on Roman and Khaos coming to terms with each other and not trying to kill each other so hard on the ice.

But how would I write that for the people in the real world where werewolves are still just a cool movie creature?

The idea fizzles a bit, but I know Roman and Slate will take care of anything slanderous.

When the second period ends, I have to pee, so Khaos comes with me. "Can you go to the bathroom too so it isn't so obvious you're literally escorting me to the bathroom?" I ask with a sarcastic smile, but seriously.

When we get to the bathrooms, the usual roles have reversed, and there is a line out the door for the men's room, and I walk right in to my stall.

I guess there aren't as many hockey gals as there are guys. That's just because they haven't watched these guys play yet.

I wash my hands and head back out. It looks like Khaos made it into the bathroom but hasn't come back out yet, so I pull out my phone to text Zoey.

> I miss your face!
>
> When we get back to town will you come over for a weekend or something?
>
> I'm having withdrawals!

I smile to myself and tuck my phone away when I notice a guy walking straight towards me. I look down and make sure not to make eye contact or engage in any way, but he stops right beside me and says, "Hey, beautiful."

"I-I'm sorry, I'm just waiting for someone," I just barely get out.

"That's okay, how about you come watch the game with me? I got the best seats in the house."

Um, okay, first off, I definitely have the best seat. Secondly, there's no way he didn't see Roman skate to me at the beginning or the three times he scored a goal.

"Um, I'm sorry. No, thank you," I squeak.

"Awe, come on. A cute thing like you deserves someone who can give her attention, not some busy and famous hockey player."

Okay, so he knows I'm with Roman, and he seriously thinks I'd rather leave with him? HA!

"I said, no, thank you," I say with more confidence this time, only he doesn't like that, and he snatches me by my wrist and starts to drag me away. I cry out with my wolf snarling beneath my skin.

"Let go of m—"

Before I can finish my sentence, Khaos is here. In a single second, he carefully extracts my wrist from the man's grip and then, not carefully at all, slams the man against the wall.

"The lady said no. Do you have a hearing problem, rogue?" He growls in the man's face.

The guy thought he was tough stuff, but the way he flinches at Khaos' words makes me smile.

"What do you mean by 'rogue?'" I interrupt.

"When a werewolf isn't loyal to an alpha, they don't have a pack and are therefore considered rogues. They also have a reputation for being without morals," he explains with another growl.

My eyes narrow, and I turn to the man. "You were going to take me, weren't you?" I expect the panic to rise, but knowing I'm safe and can confront this one brings me a sense of peace, and the anger swallows any ounce of fear.

He doesn't say anything, and a crowd is beginning to gather.

Khaos leans in close to the man, and I think he says, "You'll answer her question if you want to see daylight tomorrow."

The man's eyes widen in alarm, and he nods furiously, still refusing to say it out loud.

"You tell whoever hired you that it's not going to happen again. And we will find them."

He throws the man at least five feet away. He lands on the ground with a loud thud, drawing the rest of the attention in the area.

"Nothing to see here, folks; the man didn't understand the word 'no' when she told him," Khaos explains clearly, and the crowd mumbles at him for saving the day but dissipates. A guard comes up, and Khaos gives him the rundown on what happened. This guard is also a werewolf because Khaos goes on to explain that the man is a rogue and describes the man's scent.

The adrenaline of my earlier anger and bravery slowly seeps from my body the whole way back to our seats.

"Leera, look at me, are you okay?" Khaos asks with worry.

I look at him, but I can't tell him I'm okay. "If you weren't here, I would have been taken again..." I crumple into my seat just in time to see Roman wearing a similar look of worry on his gorgeous face.

Why can't people just leave me alone?

"I can't tell him what's going on either because we're not within the same pack; he'll have to wait until after the game for us to fill him in," Khaos says, catching the deadly stare coming from Roman on the ice.

I just have to make it through one more period. I tell myself on repeat for a few minutes.

Khaos looks torn between hunting the man down and dismembering him and trying to console me. He's obviously not a man that deals much with feelings because he gets all uncomfortable and unsure of himself. It would almost be funny if people weren't trying to kill me.

When the game is finally over, Khaos takes me to Roman, and the second he clears the locker room door, I fling myself at him.

He easily pulls my body into his and breathes in my scent from the crook of my neck. I'm surrounded by the comforting notes of cherry and leather when I pull away to look at him, wishing I could use the bond to tell him everything without having to *say it*.

Why can't I just enjoy one of his games without some kind of bullshit throwing everything off course?

He seems to forget Khaos was with me, and when he notices the hint of worry on his face, his body tenses against mine, and not in the fun way.

"What the fuck happened?" he growls at Khaos. I lean into him, resting my hand on the side of his face, pulling his eye contact, and focusing it back towards me.

"Roman, he saved me," I almost whimper with the reality of what occurred. "A man tried to take me. He came up to me, pretending to hit on me, but then he tried to drag me away. Khaos stopped him and said he was some kind of rogue."

The rest of the guys are coming out of the locker room now. Roman scoops me up into his arms, cradling me against his chest, and he clearly mentally tells everyone it's time to go, with Khaos following along just behind Roman and me.

When we finally make it to the parking lot, Roman, Khaos, and I pile into one car, while the others take the second. They can be updated telepathically, where Khaos and I cannot.

"The guy reeked of lingering dark magic, and he was definitely a hired rogue. I told him to go running back to his boss and tell them we're coming for whoever the fuck they are. I think it's time you filled me in on some obviously missing details.

33
ROMAN

I knew I should have filled Khaos in completely on what all had transpired. I really meant to, but I didn't think we'd have to worry about another kidnapping attempt already. Even though I was obviously worried enough that I ended up calling Khaos to request his assistance. I start the car for the short drive back to the hotel, and I begin to fill him in.

"We don't know why, but it has something to do with my father."

Khaos takes the news about as well as I did. I can feel his wolf trying to force a shift. "What the fuck does your father want with Leera?" he asks through gritted teeth.

"To kill me, I'm in the way of something of his..." Leera admits softly. "I heard him telling one of the kidnappers when they thought I was still knocked out from being drugged."

"What the fuck do you mean in the way of something?"

"We don't have all the details yet, but we believe it has something to do with why I was arranged to marry India. A couple months ago, she and my father came to dinner to tell me that she and I would be taking the thrones if the heir wasn't found." The thought alone still makes my blood boil. "What we don't know is why. Judging from India's reactions, we thought it was just a power move. But with new information from a local white witch, it seems there may be more going on than we could have ever anticipated."

"Goddess," Khaos sighs. "Are the King and Queen involved?"

"Not that we could find. So far the only ones involved are my father, India's father, and India."

"Isn't India's father the King's advisor? So is he doing the King's dirty work or going behind his back?" he questions.

"I have to assume that he's going behind his back. I've spent a great deal of time with the King, and he's a good man. He cares for his people. I don't think he would do anything other than what he's always done. I don't know. Something just feels off. Like we're missing a really big puzzle piece."

"W-wait...what if...oh, god!" Leera starts sobbing in the passenger seat just as I park the car, finally back at the hotel.

"Leera, baby, what's wrong? What is it?"

"Wh-what if my p-parents were killed because of me t-too?" she wails.

I want to tell her she's wrong and that her parents were just in an accident, but I don't know if I could even believe myself at this point.

34
Leera

Why has my life turned into such a complete and total shit show?

After the game the other night, I was so upset that Roman hired a plane to take us home. Us being Roman, the other starting five Predators, and me.

Khaos went to check on his pack in Maine before the next Vultures game.

As soon as we got home, he rushed upstairs and put together a candlelit bubble bath for me. It was the sweetest thing ever as it was, but being Roman, he took it further and called Zoey and planned a surprise video call, Disney movie, and bestie date for me. He left me alone to get settled in and chit-chat with Zoey. Then he came back with snacks and hot cocoa.

It's getting harder and harder not to tell this man I love him. I'll lose the war with myself soon enough. I just want it to be right. Not a moment shrouded in the constant shadows following us around.

After my bath, I thought I felt better, but the waves of grief kept slamming back into me.

I thought I had made peace with the loss of my parents, but that was when I thought that I lost them to some kind of freak accident.

The thought that they're no longer here with me is *because* of me feels like a new kind of hell.

When I finally crawl into bed with Roman, he immediately wraps both arms around me and molds my body to his. His face moves directly to the bend in my neck as he says, "I'm so sorry, Leera. I wish there was more that I could do. I wish I could take this pain away and bring them back to you. You don't deserve to feel that kind of pain."

I can feel the pain of his own experiences with loss radiating off of him. I wriggle in his hold until I've turned over to face him, running my fingers through his hair.

"Neither did you. Everything happens for a reason. I don't understand that reason right now, but someday I will. Until then, I just have to keep going…and you do."

He pulls his eyebrows together, causing the lines in his face to ripple his forehead when he asks, "I do what?"

I take my thumb and smooth out his scowl when I say, "Take my pain away." I kiss the end of his nose, roll back over in his embrace, and fall into a fitful sleep.

For the first time in what feels like a lot longer than it's really been, I wake to the smell of coffee, and my heart clenches.

I take a moment to allow the pain of yesterday to wash over me. I give in to the grief and allow the tears to fall. I don't want to hold it all in until I combust. So I'll continue to let myself feel the loss of them until it doesn't hurt so badly.

Just as the sniffles subside, Roman flings himself through the doorframe with wild worry in his eyes. "What's wrong? Are you okay?"

I give him a weak smile and nod. "I will be."

"Look, Sunshine, I wish we could postpone the trip to the pack tomorrow, but I don't think your wolf is going to wait another moon cycle. Being with the pack in nature is the best way to go through your first shift," he explains softly.

"No, I know. I want to go. I know you can't tell right this second, but I'm actually really excited and…"

"And what?" he presses.

"Well, I guess I'm also a little nervous. I've never met a whole pack of werewolves. It's more than that, though. These wolves aren't just people, they'll be like my family. They'll look up to me. I know nothing about being a Luna. What if I'm not good enough?" I mean to keep the last question to myself, but it just comes out, causing Roman to growl.

"You have absolutely nothing to be worried about. They're going to love you. Like the rest of us, they don't stand a chance," he follows up with a crooked smile on his face. "This trip isn't about you immediately taking over the duties of a Luna or anything other than you and your wolf."

I can feel her excitement beneath my skin.

I can't wait to meet you.

I look into his eyes with all the strength and happiness I can muster.

"I'm ready."

35
India

It's so good to come back to Zabella, where everyone knows exactly who I am. Not that I haven't built a brand and an awareness in the human world, but that shit takes a lot of work. Being the daughter of the King's advisor, everyone knows my name and reputation.

I was raised in the castle like a princess. It's only right that I become a queen. I'm not as excited about the responsibilities, but the title and the crown will be worth it all.

Now, it's just a matter of sorting out the whole Roman-doesn't-want-to-be-my-king business.

I was tired of talking to my father over the phone, so I figured it would just be easier if I came home for a bit and surprised him with a visit.

As my heels click on the white and gold marble floors of the castle, I'm plagued with so many fond memories in these halls.

Why am I the bad guy for wanting something I've always deserved?

My father raised me to be a queen, and I won't let him down

either.

When I reach his room, the door is cracked open.

Just before I push through the doors, I hear him shouting, but I can only make out a few words, "After all this time...it's not possible...we've come too far..." So I move closer to the wall and really focus on listening. I don't use my wolf's strengths very often, so it takes me a minute to really tune in to his conversation.

When I've heard the end of the conversation, my stomach is in knots, and I feel like I'm going to throw up.

How could they do this?

I just wanted to be a queen.

I *never* wanted *that*.

I kick my shoes off and sprint out of the castle.

I have to get out of here.

I have to do something.

They can't do this to me!

36
Leera

We spent the rest of the day just doing our own things before going to the pack.

Roman and I vowed to allow ourselves another normal day where we forget about wolves and witches and kidnappings and parents and just get to be "Roman and Leera." Those days are so few and far between, but I think they might be my favorites. Sure, the opulence is nice on occasion, but at the end of the day, lives are built in the little moments.

Benny and Andrei spent the day helping Slate continue his research, trying to find any new information they can regarding my kidnapping or Roman's father's movements or motives.

The twins have been staking out the neighborhood development where I was found to see if they can capture anyone to be questioned or any other clues to help the others with their research.

Miss Tilly has been all in a tizzy because she hasn't really been away from the townhouse since she moved in with the guys. We convinced her to come to the pack with us. I think she thinks she's going to come back, and the townhouse will magically be in shambles without her presence. It makes my heart happy that she's coming with us, though. I've become quite fond of her and our conversations while she lets me help in the kitchen.

Elder Meredith, Miss Tilly's sister, will be coming with us to visit the pack as well, but she'll stay with the pack when we come back home. She's been staying to visit since my arrival, and I hope Miss Tilly isn't too lonely once she's gone again.

Healer Jeanine left while we were in Dover. She wanted to make sure she was prepared for everyone's first shifts this evening.

I'm now packing my bags for tomorrow, filled with a mixture of excitement and anxiety. I'm so excited to meet the pack and the pups and my wolf. I'm worried of how they'll feel about me and how shifting for the first time will feel. When the guys do it, they don't look like they're in pain, but the sounds it makes are grotesque.

Speaking of sounds, all of a sudden, I hear growling and maybe yelling. I follow the source of the ruckus and find a furious Roman yelling at the twins, "How the hell does she keep getting back here?"

He can't possibly mean—

You've got to be shitting me right now!

But wait, something's wrong. I can feel it.

Roman's hauling ass to the door to intercept India. How can he not feel that something's wrong? I mean, look at her.

I think it's India. It roughly looks and smells like India. I never noticed before that she smells like Easter lilies. This India, though, isn't wearing shoes, and her hair is a disaster.

"India, I told you never to come back here!" Roman roars in her face, and she doesn't even flinch.

She's looking around, begging anyone to listen to her when I approach where they're standing by the door.

I stop next to Roman and place my hand on his arm and say, "Roman, please, let her talk. Something's wrong. Can't you feel that?"

He looks at me in confusion before turning back to India and looking her over for a moment.

"I can see she's a mess, but I don't feel anything, Leera." He looks at me with calculation before it's broken by India.

"Roman, Leera, you have to believe me. I didn't know!" she wails. "I never w-would have wanted any of it. I swear, I didn't know!"

She's sobbing now and almost falls into a heap on the floor when I lurch forward and catch her head before it hits the ground. "Roman, help me. Bring her to the couch."

He nods and does what I ask but doesn't say anything because he's clearly communicating with his men.

"Get me an ice pack, a warm, wet rag, and a glass of water, please."

"I'm on it, dearie," Miss Tilly says, flitting to the kitchen after materializing from nowhere.

India's inconsolable; her body still being wracked with sobs when Miss Tilly returns with my requests.

I quickly take the rag and run it over India's face, hoping to calm her while Miss Tilly moves to check on her feet that look like they might be bleeding a bit.

"Shhhh, India, you're okay. Can you sit up a bit so I can place the ice pack on your neck, and can you take a drink of this water? They'll help the panic."

She listens easily enough and allows me to help her.

"Okay, now, India, look at me. Keep your eyes on me and copy my breathing."

When she's holding my gaze, I take an exaggerated breath in, hold it for ten seconds, holding my fingers up for the countdown, and then slowly release the breath. We do this together on repeat for five breaths before she finally calms down.

"Thank you for that, Leera. Really. I'm so fucking s-sorry for e-everything," she begins but starts to lose control of her emotions again.

"Hey, focus. I accept your apology, but we can't help if you don't tell us what's going on."

While I've been working to calm India on the couch, the men have all gathered at the giant island, giving us space but still listening to what's going on.

"I w-I went home to Z-Zabella. I wanted to c-confront my f-father about what w-we were going to d-do because I wanted s-so badly to be q-queen." She's barely keeping it together while she gets this out, so I'm just listening and giving her the space she needs. She takes a short break, then a deep breath, and continues, "When I got to Daddy's office, he was yelling. I d-don't know who he was t-talking to because I d-didn't go in. At f-first I couldn't hear, s-so I got closer, and I..." Another small sob escapes her. We wait, some more patiently than others, for her to continue. I can feel Roman's energy getting prickly.

"What is it, India? Let us help," I ask softly.

"I just hope it's not too late," she whispers.

37
ROMAN

On any other day, my patience would have dried up by now. I'm barely keeping it together because, even though Leera is doing an amazing job and I want to see her in action, this isn't how the men and I get information. We don't calm them and ask nicely. After everything she's put Leera through, I should be surprised she's able to be that compassionate with her. But it's just her. It's who Leera is. It's her presence and spirit. She's a Luna down to her soul.

With that thought, I find myself able to relax and wait a little longer before jumping in.

"Too late for what?" Leera asks, offering India another sip of water.

India accepts the water before she visibly works to gather herself for whatever she has to say. I straighten myself in preparation for the weight of what could have brought her here like this.

She speaks slowly and clearly when she says, "I heard him say that they were working with dark witches. That they will never stop until they've seized control of Zabella, Sabbax, the human realm, and..."

"And what, India? I'm losing my patience," I snarl before I can stop myself.

Leera narrows her eyes at me before returning to India. "It's okay. What are they planning?"

She looks Leera right in the eyes when she says, "He said that they have to do whatever it takes to complete the *prophecy*. He said they're coming for Roman. He said they're done playing nice. They'll start killing innocent people, no matter the species, until you do whatever they need for the prophecy to be met. I didn't even know there was a prophecy. I-I swear, I didn't know about all of that. I thought this was just about me being queen. I had no idea it was more than the throne. I never th...I never thought they were capable of *this.*"

All I can say without losing my shit is, "When."

She shakes her head. "He didn't say. I came as quickly as I heard."

"Why now? You've been working with them for a long fucking time, India. I'd say probably just over five hundred years, if I had to guess." Her flinch answers that question. "You knew he killed her, didn't you?"

"Yes, I knew, okay! They've been training me for this my entire life! I just wanted to be a queen! Yes, I wanted you to myself, but the Goddess had other plans. Obviously. But I don't know how many people they're planning to kill or have already killed. I don't know anything about a prophecy. I don't know what they plan to do with the power. He said..." She chokes on another broken sob. "He said that since I couldn't do my part, I was no longer needed, and they might as well get rid of me too!"

Now it all makes sense. India has only ever cared about herself and the crown. But she only finally told us what's going on and came to us because her life is now on the line as well.

"Roman, we have to do something," Leera pleads.

I raise a single eyebrow at her. "Why should we help her? She made her bed."

"Roman Razboinic," Leera scolds as she stands to her full height and plants her hands on her hips. "While she is obviously far from one of my favorite people, there is a big difference between wanting to knock some sense into someone and letting then die when we can do something about it."

"Roman, please. I promise to stay out of your way or help you all in any way I can; just please don't let them do this. I'll be a better wolf. Whatever you want, I'll do it. Please," India begs.

I snarl to myself at the thought of helping her. After everything she's been a part of, *can I really help her?*

Leera will never forgive you if you just let them kill her, Benny replies. Apparently, I said that part to my men.

What do all of you think? I intentionally ask them this time.

Slate's the first to respond, *We'll have to help her, or we're no better than they are. She may also have more useful information, like why Avram's scent is never found.*

Shit, he's right.

I roll my neck in irritation. "We'll help you, but not at the risk of Leera or our lives. We're leaving for the pack's full moon ceremony tomorrow morning, so we'll have to find somewhere for you to stay. You're not staying here without anyone."

"I'll ask Khaos if she can stay with him or his pack while we're gone. We'll only be gone a couple of days," Leera pipes up, and the confusion on India's face would be comical if it wasn't for the bomb she had just dropped on us.

I nod. It's not going to be as easy as she thinks. If India truly wants our protection, she's going to have to provide information, and she's going to have to swear her loyalty. Not to me. To Leera. She'll have to create a pack bond with her, preventing her from betraying her in any way. We'll address that when we return from the pack.

"India, we have information that we need from you. We'll get that and handle any other concerns when we return. Leera, can you go ahead and get in touch with Khaos so we can confirm she has somewhere to stay?"

I don't like this, Andrei chimes in.

We just don't like her, the twins add in unison.

I don't either, but Slate and Benny are right. We can't stoop to their level, and Leera would never forgive us if we just let them kill her. No matter how much easier that would make my life.

"I'll do anything you all want; just please don't let them kill me!" India continues to cry.

"I'm on it," Leera announces as she pulls her phone from her pocket to call her brother.

Slate takes his laptop and moves to sit on the floor in front of India to get as much information from her while she's still agreeable.

Benny hands me a glass of whiskey as I take a seat at the barstool next to him on the island.

"How did life get so fucked up so quickly?" I ask no one in particular.

"Eh, it was getting a bit boring there for a while; we needed something to spice things up a bit," Benny chuckles. "I mean, let's face it, Boss, before Leera showed up, you were only existing for hockey and the pack. You weren't happy. You were barely even living."

He's right, but I won't say that, so I just grunt in agreement and take a swig from my whiskey.

"Right now, we need to focus first on Leera's likely shift tomorrow tonight. It's going to be a lot for her, and with her going all her life without shifting, I don't know how painful it will be."

Benny nods.

"Did you pack the things I asked for?"

"Yep," he responds, popping the P for emphasis just when Leera comes back into the room with that smile on her face that makes my heart stop.

"Khaos wasn't happy about it, but he agreed to let her stay at his pack's house until we get back. He said if she'll catch a flight, he'll pick her up from the airport. Make sure she doesn't use her credit cards or anything."

Nodding to myself, I say, "Slate, can you throw together a fake identity in time so she doesn't have to use her name either? That way, they can't track her."

"I think so, Boss. Let me start on that now then."

With a plan of action in place, we set to finish getting ready for tomorrow.

38
Leera

Today is the day.

The day my life will change forever.

I mean, don't get me wrong, this last year has irrevocably changed me in more ways than I care to discuss, but today is on a totally different level.

Tonight, to be exact.

Tonight, my body will totally transfigure into the body of a wolf. My wolf. My soul. If only people really knew some of us actually do have spirit animals.

I asked Roman what the full moon ceremony usually looks like so that I know what to expect.

He let me know that tonight will be a special ceremony. In addition to any other wolves that will experience their first shift, there is also a new wolf wanting to join the pack, which is a separate process that will take place as the sun sets.

We're on the way now—just Roman, Miss Tilly, Elder Meredith, and me, along with all of our luggage. The rest of the guys chose to make a nice long run of it in their wolf forms after they dropped India off at the airport.

When we arrive, I will be introduced to the pack, not formally, just in general. We'll spend the day helping around to prepare for the evening. Lots of cooking, firewood gathering, and so much more.

As the sun begins its final descent, the wolf wishing to join the pack will have to pledge their loyalty to Roman. When a pack bond is created, it's slightly similar to a mate bond in that it requires the bite to connect the wolf to the alpha. It's what grants them the ability to communicate telepathically with the rest of the pack, but it also creates a bond that prevents the wolf from ever betraying their alpha. In the event of a betrayal, the bond will be severed, alerting the alpha, similarly to the death of a pack member, and the alpha's mark will fade.

Apparently, some alphas require their packs to accept a much larger pack-bond mark on their neck, like a mate bond. Roman, however, believes that the intimacy of that bite should be saved for mates. He marks his pack members on their hands, in the meaty section between the thumb and forefinger.

I hadn't noticed the marks on any of his men or the women, but when he finished telling me about it, Miss Tilly leaned forward to let me see her mark. I was expecting it just to look like a dog bite, in all honesty, but it was so much more. A small gasp escaped me when I saw it, and I felt a tingling sense of recognition that I couldn't place.

I held her hand in mine, just in awe of what I saw. I ran my finger over the intricacy of Roman's mark designated by the Moon Goddess. You can see where his canines broke the flesh, just above each knuckle. Then seeming to sprout from where the incisors left their mark are pale lines twisting and swirling together to form a web of a design in the center. It's gorgeous. I wasn't expecting that at all. Which led me to ask whether mate bond marks are just bites or if they create a mark as well.

Chosen mates just have a bite mark and sometimes a small design of some kind. Fated mate bonds can become larger, more intricate designs. Elder Meredith told me of all the marks she'd seen in her time. They can range in all kinds of natural colors, from reds, browns, blacks, pinks, and whites. The designs themselves can't truly be described without having seen them. They're not images. Similar to the pack bond, they're a pattern of lines. Some are soft and sensual, others are sharp and jagged; it has a lot to do with the souls. They are usually a reflection of the one who wears it.

In a fated mate bond, they usually aren't even the same between each wolf. Each mate may have their own design that either represents themselves or their mate.

When I finally finished asking all my questions about that portion, he continued to explain the rest.

Once the sun fully set beneath the sky, they would light the bonfire and wait. Some wolves shift immediately, while others could take hours. There's no way to tell when it will begin or how long the first shift will take.

That's the part that I fear the most, but the soft caress beneath my skin reminds me how worth it this will be.

There are no rules as to what form the pack attends the ceremony in, so there will be wolves and people milling about. Additionally, not everyone is required to attend; it's a very casual and voluntary affair. But with each transformation, the pack will feel the shift. When the young ones shift for the first time, that's what connects them to the pack bond. They'll have their telepathic communication, and their mark will appear without a bite because they were born from two pack members. They will not have the bite mark, just the pack mark, and they can choose to accept their Alpha's bite when they come of age.

After someone has shifted, there is also no official process for how long they will remain in their wolf form. The younger ones especially like to run and play until they collapse into sleep. Some wolves go for a run, and their families often join them. Some shift, then prefer to shift right back to continue practicing the shift. It's about connecting with your wolf and doing what feels right.

After almost four hours in the car, I'm just staring out the window, appreciating the changing colors of the leaves, my mind racing faster than the car itself. I'm feeling all the feelings when the car begins to slow.

Roman flashes me a smile that should be illegal. Hooking his thumb over his shoulder, he explains, "We'll have to take that from here. There aren't driving trails into the park as far as we're going."

There's a four-seated ATV that looks similar to a dune buggy but camouflaged.

"How long does it take to get to the pack from here?" I ask, buckling myself in.

"About twenty minutes, give or take," Miss Tilly informs me, and she was right. Nineteen minutes later—yes, I was counting—we pull up to one of the most gorgeous places I've ever seen.

In the midst of this massive forest, there's a clearing and a lake surrounded by trees. The homes that look like small log cabins with green roofs are built on the edge of the tree line. It's seriously so breathtaking; it looks like what you'd see in a high-end mountain resort where someone would go to unwind and reset their mind.

I'm definitely gawking, and I don't even care. That's not even all there is. There are a few larger buildings in various areas, a dock extending into the lake, and even a few treehouses built into the giant trees.

It feels like I've been transported to another world.

In the center of all of it, I can see a ring of large boulders that they must use as the border to the bonfire for their full moon ceremonies.

"Roman, this is...I can't even tell you because nothing I say will do it justice."

The smile on his face reflects the pride he feels for his pack.

Just as I lean into him, his presence is known, and the pack begins to make their way to us. Here goes nothing!

39
ROMAN

Seeing her here, on our land, among our pack, is a moment I will tuck away and save forever. The awe written all over her face when we arrived made me feel a sense of pride that I haven't felt in a very long time.

I've always cared for my pack and what we created here, but I don't think I've really allowed myself to enjoy it or take credit for it for so long. My arranged marriage was causing me more unhappiness than I even realized. Bringing her out here only happened a few times because she hated it so much that all she did was bitch. She never saw the beauty in our land or people. To avoid those feelings, I, unfortunately, had to avoid my pack.

What's that thing I heard those human men say once... "Hindsight is always twenty-twenty?" Or something like that. It's incredibly true and humbling.

As the pack comes to greet us, I see the flicker of fear on Leera's face, but I don't even acknowledge it. I know everyone will love her. They won't even be able to help it. She'll smile or laugh, and they'll be another casualty to her beautiful soul.

I see my men bringing up the rear of the group, still in wolf form, and I know exactly what they're doing, and she sees them coming.

A giggle escapes her. "Are those the guys?"

A grunt is my only response as they sprint past the rest of our pack coming to greet us, stopping just before they barrel into Leera, who squeals with excitement.

"Wait, wait, wait! I want to see if I can guess who is who! Is that okay?" she turns to ask me.

"Sweetheart, you can do whatever you please with my men; actually, no. No, you can't. But yes, guess away." I swear, Benny's wolf snickers at me.

Her cheeks turn pink, and her eyes narrow at me for a moment before she returns to her task at hand.

"Sorry, boys, it's a little obvious," she says as she points to the twins' gray wolves, causing them to whimper.

Next, she points to the large black wolf. He's the only wolf whose tail isn't wagging. "Slate, is that you?"

His wolf nods and walks away, clearly ready to move on.

She's down to a large cinnamon-colored wolf and a brindled wolf. Both wolves are wagging their tails and seem to be smiling. She looks back and forth between them for a moment before she closes her eyes and slowly turns to the brindled wolf. "Andrei?"

Benny and I share a look that says I'll most definitely be asking what that was later.

Andrei bows his head and then lays down.

Then there's just Benny, and I should warn her, but I don't.

Before she can turn to fully face him, he barrels into her and licks her entire face.

"OH, MY GAWD! BENJAMIN...what is his last name

again, so I can yell at him properly?" she screeches.

"Bucur," I laugh.

"BENJAMIN BUCUR, YOU CAN NOT GO AROUND SLOBBERING ALL OVER PEOPLE!" she hollers at him, but she's laughing.

Just as Benny prances off, the pack begins to reach us.

Miss Tilly pulls a handkerchief from her pocket and hands it to Leera to clean up the drool dripping from her face.

The pack gathers around us, offering a respectful distance, allowing me to introduce Leera at once, "Hello, everyone! I want to introduce you to my mate, Leera. The Goddess has returned her soul to me within this lifetime, which was confirmed by Elder Meredith," I announce to clear any confusion as most of the pack knows my history.

Elder Meredith looks across the span of faces and simply nods.

Leera's blushing, smiling, and offering sweet little waves to the pack members.

Everyone is smiling. "Please, let us help prepare for the full moon ceremonies. Leera and I will make our rounds and do our best to meet everyone through the course of the day."

Everyone smiles, waves, and begins to lead the children away, but I always play with the children when I arrive. "If it's okay with the parents, I would still like to play with the pups for a bit before I get to work."

The parents laugh and tell their young ones to behave themselves as they walk away.

With the parents out of the way, I look back to the children to find them in awe of Leera, who's also staring at them with hearts in her eyes.

"You're so pretty, like a princess," the young girl who hugged me the last time I was here compliments Leera, causing her to blush all over.

"Thank you," she squeaks. "I'm Leera. What's your name?" she asks as she kneels to the children's level.

"My name is Penelope," she answers, taking Leera's hand and leading her to a log off to the side. "We should sit here; the boys like to wrestle with Alpha when he gets here."

It's at that moment that I realize that she is the only little girl in the pack. I smile at them perched on the log before mayhem ensues. I allow myself to be tackled to the ground by little people and pups alike. When they've got me down and covered, I shift, and my wolf breaks through the pile of children and pups to play.

The smile on Leera's face while she watches us and chats with Penelope shoots straight through to my heart.

Is this what having my own family would be like?

Would Leera want to live with the pack and be part of our community?

Could I feel this kind of freeing happiness every day?

I don't know how long we wrestle, and I don't care. We go until the pups are pooped out, and we all collapse onto the ground, earning us a few more snickers from the girls.

My wolf is panting, but we're happy. Leera makes her way over and scratches us behind the ear, and fuck, if it doesn't feel amazing.

"You're just a great big softie, aren't you?" she asks in a mushy baby voice that would be patronizing if she wasn't so damn cute.

I decide to follow Benny's lead and lick up her whole face.

"OH! ROMAN RAZBOINIC!" she squeals again.

Penelope wags her finger in front of my snout. "Uh, uh, uh, you're in trouble now."

Leera's laughing again.

Using my muzzle, I pull her into me. She plops onto the ground, and I wrap myself around her. She rubs her face all through my fur, giving back my slobbery kisses before sinking into me.

Little Penelope's mother comes to collect her to help with chores, and Leera smiles and waves in return.

"I can't wait to meet my wolf. I'm sure you can't either. Not you, Roman, but your wolf. Will my wolf look the same as your last mate's? Or will she reflect me?"

I can feel my wolf's love for her as much as my own. Even with me getting Leera back, it still doesn't change the fact that he has gone so long without her wolf. I hadn't thought about whether the wolf would be the same. Since our wolves usually match us physically in some way, and Leera and Imogen are so different, I would assume the wolves would be different too. It's the souls that continue moving on.

I allow myself a few more minutes to nuzzle her before nudging her to hop up. Once she's up, I nod towards the rock where I had someone from the pack drop off a cloak for me. I don't think Leera's ready for me to just walk around stark naked...yet anyway.

Once I've shifted and donned the cloak, I turn back to her. "Let's help everyone get ready for this evening," I suggest, as I drop a kiss to her knuckles.

40
Leera

We've spent all day helping the pack prepare for tonight, and we're about an hour away from beginning the acceptance ceremony for the new wolf. We met and spoke with him already, and he seemed really nice. He was raised in a pack in the south, but when their alpha passed without an heir, it tore the pack apart. Friends and brothers turned on each other, so he made his way north. When he heard of Roman's pack, he continued his journey here.

I have never seen so much food in one place in all my life. It makes sense, though; I've seen how much food six of them can eat; I can't imagine having to cook for an entire pack every day.

The wood the men collected for the bonfire is stacked into a teepee shape that's taller than me in the center of the rock circle that I saw when we came in. With the wood piled that high, that bonfire is going to be humongous.

I'm starting to get a bit jittery from nerves, but I just keep reminding myself how worth it this will be. It almost feels like the jitters aren't just my nerves. It feels as though it's also partially a result of my wolf's excitement.

I'm still so sorry you've been locked up all my life. I truly can't wait to meet you.

She huffs and brushes her calming fur beneath my skin.

I've so enjoyed meeting so many amazing people…or werewolves? I'm not sure what the appropriate protocol is when referencing everyone. *Add that to my list of werewolf questions.* The women of the pack have been so nice, allowing me to help and just talking with me like I've been here all along.

Penelope has spent the day glued to my side, after approving it with her mother, of course. Her and Roman took me on the grand tour, and it was so much more than I ever expected.

The Twilight werewolves weren't immortal, so they didn't have the time and resources to build something like all of this.

I have to stop comparing, but it still makes me laugh. I can't believe this is real life.

I've been taking pictures of how beautiful everything is too. The people working. The trees. The lake. Roman working with his shirt off. *Whew.* I'm so glad I brought my camera. It also feels like having my parents here with me for the big day.

Having finished all the chores, Penelope and I have been braiding wildflower crowns for each other and any of the women who would like one, but we stop when we see Roman approaching us. "I hate to spoil the fun, but it's almost time to begin the acceptance ceremony. Would you be by my side?" he asks with his hand extended to me like a fairytale prince.

"I'd be honored." And my goofy ass curtsies with a snort, causing him to throw his head back and laugh.

When we've pulled ourselves together and make eye contact, the world threatens to fall away and leave just the two of us. The moment is quickly broken when little Penelope takes Roman's other hand to pull herself from the ground where we were sitting.

"Thank you, kind sir," she says with a dramatic curtsy of her own, then skips over to where her mother is standing, and we break into another small fit of laughter.

Roman takes my hand and leads me to where everyone is gathering by the still unlit bonfire, just as the sun touches the horizon. The rest of his men are waiting near the front as well. Benny winks and smiles his contagious smile, making mine grow wider.

Once everyone gathers around, Roman speaks, "Good evening! I first want to thank everyone for allowing me and Leera to help prepare for this evening. I hope to be much more present in pack activities moving forward."

He stops for a moment to smile at me, and I know I've got to be red as a tomato.

"We have a new wolf joining our pack this evening. I think everyone else has gotten to know him well since his arrival. Thomas, can you join us?"

The group parts to allow him easier access to join us at the front of the space.

"Thomas, do you vow to honor and protect this pack, participate in traditions, and remain loyal to our people and myself?"

"I swear," he answers and holds his hand out to Roman.

Roman takes his hand and does this weird move with his jaw, bringing his large canines out like magic, before leaning in and biting the flesh between his thumb and forefinger, just like he described. It begins to bleed, but Roman licks the wound, healing it. There's a small murmur through the crowd, and I assume it's from the physical effects of adding another member to their pack. Roman said they can physically feel it, more similar to a family bond, as it's not as strong as a mate bond.

Thomas nods, as though to bow to Roman, and Roman claps him on the shoulder in that weird man-hug thing men do. They then turn to the crowd. "Everyone, let's formally welcome Thomas into the pack!" Roman bellows, and everyone claps and whoops.

Now that the ceremony is over and the sun is slowly sinking, some men begin to light the bonfire, and the women begin bringing all the food out of the community building. I smile at Roman before running over to help.

It probably takes us thirty minutes to carry out what's basically a massive feast of smoked meats, veggies, salads, pasta, fruit, and homemade breads. I haven't seen so much homemade food in one place, well, ever. When it's all laid out and Penelope has gone through and put a spoon or tongs in each bowl and platter, Miss Tilly yells, "Come and get it!" The twins start running towards the tables when she levels them with a look. "Children first!"

They pout in jest and kick rocks like scolded children.

The kids and pups scurry to the tables, some dragging their mothers, and begin making plates. A couple of them try to woo their parents into letting them have dessert first. Roman comes up to my side, and I lean into him, just taking it all in.

"I love it here," I tell him breathlessly. "Your pack, the lands—it feels like the real world, except none of my problems can reach us here."

He wraps one arm around me, pulling me closer, and kisses the top of my head. "I've always felt at peace here, but nothing compares to being here with you."

I turn into him, resting my hand on his heart. "I'm beginning to understand that my peace seems to be wherever you are."

Just as I lean in to kiss him, Benny pops out from behind Roman. "New guy seems okay, yeah?" He's smiling like he knows exactly what he just did, and he narrowly dodges a smack to the back of the head. "Gotta be quicker than that, old man!"

"Can we eat now? I'm starved." And on cue, my stomach rumbles.

Slate reaches the tables as we do, and it's weird not to see him tethered to an electronic of some kind. "What, no research tonight?"

I swear, he almost smiled! I saw his lip twitch!

"Unfortunately not, there isn't cell service out here, and the only internet that works remotely well is the hardwired stuff," he explains with a shrug.

"That makes sense. I hadn't even thought of that. Well, as a pack, you don't really need cell phones since you can communicate without them," I rationalize out loud.

Both men nod, loading their plates with enough food to feed, well, a wolf.

We probably have about ten minutes before the sunset is complete, so we take our seats to eat around the bonfire. Everyone is smiling. Well, except Slate. But even he's happy; he just doesn't show it on the outside. It doesn't make sense, but it's like I can feel it. The happiness.

It's like when you're driving down the road in the desert, and it's so hot that the air in the distance looks wiggly and distorted. Like some kind of visible gas or something. It's so weird, but that's how it feels. I know that doesn't really make sense, but it's all I've got. It must have to do with the ceremonies and the bonfire.

When we've finished eating, I grab as many plates around me as I can. A few people didn't want me to take it for them, but I insisted. I want to be just like everyone else, even if I'm Roman's mate. I don't want special treatment. The trash is taken almost all the way back to the clubhouse where the food was pulled from. When I turn to walk back, the beauty of it all stops me in my tracks.

The lake in the distance, surrounded by trees older than even these wolves. The bonfire roaring to life, surrounded by people of all ages sitting, standing, and even dancing. Crickets chirping and the last lightning bugs of the year taking flight.

I forget that I was walking back to the group when Roman joins me, wrapping a shawl around my shoulders, even though I hadn't really gotten cold yet, even if it's already October.

It's already been two months into my new life, but somehow it feels like a lifetime.

"With the sun fully set, you could shift any time. Would you like to be out here with the pack, or would you like to have some privacy?" he asks with a tinge of worry in his eyes.

"I'm okay, Roman. I want to be out here with the pack, like everyone else," I tell him as strongly as I can, even though my legs kind of feel like Jello.

As we make our way back to the bonfire, one of the children hollers, and at first, I worry something is wrong, but then I realize he's shifting. Everyone grants him space. No one's staring at him. His parents are nearby, offering quiet words of encouragement. The sounds are the worst part. Hearing bones crunch and realign like that is terrifying, but I'm sure I'll get used to it someday.

After about four or five minutes, his shift is complete, and a dark chocolate little wolf is bounding around where the little boy once was. Everyone either claps or howls their encouragement. Both his and his parents' eyes are shining with pride, his mother patting away her happy tears. They shift and join him, prancing and running around, and I can't help the swell in my chest.

I could have that someday.

We find a spot to settle in and wait. Roman and I start talking about his life in Zabella. He doesn't have many fond memories, but hearing stories about another world is fascinating.

Benny is about to tell us a story of little Roman when I start to feel...something.

"R-roman I...s-something's...ahhhh!"

He scrambles from where he's sitting and kneels beside me where I've fallen to the ground. I'm getting the burning flesh feeling I got when my wolf tried to force her way out.

I vaguely notice Miss Tilly, Jeanine, and the men around me, but my eyes can't seem to focus. Another small scream rips from my lungs.

"Is she okay?" I barely hear Roman worry over the pain.

"She's fine, Alpha. Due to her age, her first shift is going to be even more uncomfortable than most."

I roll over onto all fours to try and just move through the pain coming over me in waves.

For a moment, I genuinely feel as though someone has thrown me into the bonfire; just before my body goes cold and is covered in goosebumps, I hear the first pop, causing me to cry out again.

"You've got this, Sweetheart."

Bones crunching.

"Everything's going to be okay; keep breathing."

Tendons stretching.

"You're almost there."

Fur sprouting.

"Holy shit."

For a single second, I can't hear or see anything as I feel my wolf's presence consume me, and my scream morphs into a howl of triumph.

Just as all four of my feet, *er, paws,* hit the earth, what can only be described as a shockwave courses through my body. Not only does it travel through my entire body, but it passes through my legs, into the earth, and out into the world. It blows out the entire bonfire. It brings the pack to their knees. *Why are they bowing?* This did not happen when the little boy shifted.

Everything I see through the eyes of my wolf is so much sharper. Every breath I take, I can smell everything, but...*oh my god...*the smell of cherries and leather is what I turn to, my eyes nearly rolling back in my head.

I find Roman in a state somewhere between shock and awe, his men gathered around him. Everyone but Andrei, wearing the same face as the rest of the pack.

Is something wrong with my wolf?

I look down and inspect my legs. *My fur is silver, like my hair!* I turn to check my sides when I see my tail, so I swish it back and forth and mentally beam. My wolf prances in a circle in excitement before rushing up to Roman and nuzzling him.

Then, for the appropriate payback, I serve Roman and Benny the biggest, slobberiest kisses I can, but they continue to gape at me.

I hunch down and whimper at their reactions.

Andrei snaps out of it first. "Roman, I feel I have some explaining to do."

41
ROMAN

She is the single most magnificent creature I have ever seen, but I'm in such a state of shock that I can't even properly convey that to her. Now she seems upset with me as I all but drag Andrei across the clearing so we can privately discuss what the fuck just happened.

Leera has her tail tucked between her legs like she's done something wrong. "Leera, baby, it's not you. You're fucking perfect, but"—I pull my t-shirt off over my head as I move her towards the tree—"I need you to shift back for me for just a minute. We need to have a very important discussion. Then you can shift back and spend as much time with your wolf as you'd like."

She tilts her head at me, which I interpret to mean, "And exactly how the fuck am I supposed to do that? No one told me."

"You focus on your body and will yourself back into your human form. You can tell your wolf to, and she'll help."

She plants her front paws in preparation and narrows her eyes in concentration. She shifts flawlessly, but she wasn't prepared, so she falls to the forest floor.

I immediately pull my shirt over her head, placing her arms in the holes, and scoop her into my arms. "I'm so fucking proud of you. You don't even know how breathtaking you are. The most beautiful wolf I've ever seen," I tell her as I pepper her with kisses.

She wraps her arms around my neck and kisses me hard. "It was so incredible. Did you see my fur?! It was silver like my hair!"

"We saw, my little miracle. We saw everything. Which is what we need to talk about." I set her down on a log and kneel in front of her, taking her hands in mine. "Leera, that gust that released when you shifted. That wasn't part of a normal werewolf's first shift," I tell her seriously.

Her eyes widen. "Did I–did I do something wrong?"

"No, baby, not at all. You didn't have any control over it. You see, when a wolf with royal blood shifts for the first time, it sends out basically a message to all werewolves to let them know that the royal heir has their wolf. We don't know why the Goddess does this, but the last time I felt it, we assumed the lost princess was still alive out there somewhere. Since you had never shifted before, I didn't even consider…" The words leave me as I hang my head.

All she wanted was a normal life, but now so many things are beginning to line up.

"No."

"Fucking."

"Way."

Benny and the twins chime off.

"Ha! W-what?! N-n-no. Nope. I think I know what you're saying, and, yeah, just nope. We are NOT going there," Leera demands, crossing her arms in front of her to make a giant X.

"Andrei, what part do you play in this?" I growl at him, but he's looking at Leera with tears in his eyes.

"Leera." He kneels next to her. "Do you feel it?"

Her eyes widen, then dart to meet mine before she sniffles and nods her head.

I'm whipping my head back and forth, trying to understand. "Feel what?" I snarl.

"I'm so sorry, I didn't tell you, Roman. We've had so much going on, and I kept forgetting. I swear, I wasn't keeping it f-from you," she whimpers.

I rear back in shock. "Sweetheart, don't cry. I'm not mad at you, him maybe, but just tell me what's going on."

She nods to herself. "I get the same small tugging from Andrei that I get around Khaos."

My eyes narrow, and I look at Andrei hard.

They're the same age.

He's been on some kind of mission for vengeance he couldn't talk about.

His visceral reactions when we met her, or when she was in pain or kidnapped.

The longer I look, the more they look alike.

But none of this makes sense.

"Roman, I can explain," Andrei says, breaking me from my spiraling thoughts.

"You damn well better."

"You all might want to sit down for this one."

42
ANDREI

This is it. The moment I've been waiting for. I felt the tugging, and I could tell from her confused glances that she could too, but like Roman, I couldn't allow myself to believe it until I was certain.

I knew tonight would confirm and erase any doubt.

And it did.

"I'm going to start at the beginning and explain as much as I can about the whole situation," I tell them all.

The men scoot closer, eager to find out what's going on while Leera is perched on Roman's lap, and I just hope they both don't hate me for not saying anything sooner. I had to know.

"The King and Queen had been trying to have a child for nearly a thousand years. They continued to trust in the Moon Goddess and her plans, but were also heartbroken at the constant hole they felt in their lives. About twenty years ago, they'd been dealing with rumors of an uprising and spent all their time working to protect their people and thwart any threats. While their minds were preoccupied with something other than an addition to their family, the Moon Goddess decided that would be the best time to bless them with a child. I've heard it happens to humans all the time. They were obviously thrilled at the news but worried about what would happen if the rebels found a way to harm the child."

"When the royal healer came to their chambers to check on the health of the baby, she made all servants and advisors leave, while the healer had to swear her loyalty directly to the Queen through a bond. She did this because there was not only one baby. The Queen was pregnant with twins. A blessing no other royal family had ever received from the Goddess. The King and Queen were terrified of news getting out. So, they announced they were with child, holding back the specifics. During her pregnancy, threats continued to grow."

"Why wasn't I told any of this? Why wasn't I brought home to protect them?" Roman roars, Leera patting his arm with tears rolling down her cheeks.

"Because the King knew what you'd been through. He knew why you hadn't returned to Zabella. They continued to take precautions, and they thought they could handle it."

"And they were wrong!" he continues.

"They were. Because of the growing threats, they made a plan that when the Queen went into labor, she would be with only the healer. No servants would be allowed. The day the princess was born was a magical day for our kingdom—for our kind. But she was not the only one born that day. I was born fourteen minutes before her. Our mother held us together for as long as she could before the advisors and court were demanding to see the baby. You know how awful they can be. It was decided that I would be hidden, raised in secret in case the worst should happen."

The old heaviness settles on my shoulders when she touches my arm, and it slowly dissipates.

"The night of your introduction to the kingdom, there was an attack on the Queen. We don't know if it was always their plan, but they attacked her, and they took you. They took you, and I swore I would spend my entire existence trying to find you," I choke.

"Why didn't the King and Queen just announce that they had a son and an heir to the throne?" Slate interjects.

"For fear that I, too, would be kidnapped. And so that I could do exactly as I did and find her." I turn to Roman. "Do you really think that in all the realms and all of the worlds, I found you by accident? Sure, I knew your reputation, but the last few years, I should have still been looking for her. I should have moved on. But I couldn't. It felt wrong. I know the Goddess kept me here for a reason. As the heir to the throne, I didn't want it. It didn't feel like mine. It always felt like hers. If she couldn't have it, neither would I."

Leera looks between Roman and me with wide eyes. "S-so you're sitting here telling me, in all seriousness, that not only are you my brother—not just my soul brother—but you are my..." She chokes on a sob as tears continue to trickle down her cheeks. "You're not even just my brother, you're my twin?"

I nod.

"And not only that, but ta-da, you're a fucking princess?!"

I nod.

"Shut. Up," she says in all seriousness, and everyone just stares at me.

"Leera, baby, are you okay?" Roman asks her, cupping the

side of her face.

"How the fuck am I supposed to respond to that? To any of this?" she asks, throwing her hands in the air. "As if I'm not awkward enough on my own, let's add a freaking tiara. You're joking, right? This is some kind of first shift prank, right?"

I shake my head.

She lifts herself off his lap and slowly walks towards me, arm outstretched. When she reaches me, I close my eyes, and her touch on my cheek sends shockwaves through my body, and my wolf howls.

"It's true," she gasps.

All I can do is nod, another tear slipping through my eyes.

43
Leera

I sit on the log, staring out at the clearing in complete and total shock at the giant, steaming pile of shit my life has become in the last year.

I feel like one of those cartoon waitresses trying to get back to the kitchen with the dirty dishes, but people just keep throwing more on the pile. Now, instead of just trying to get to the kitchen, I have to get there without dropping or breaking anything.

I was slightly terrified yet so excited for my first shift.

It felt otherworldly to be united with my wolf.

Until it all came crashing down.

Again.

Because that's what my life does.

I should be enjoying my wolf. Running with Roman and the men.

Nope.

Not me.

I find out I'm some twisted Twilight version of Rapunzel.

I guess in some ways it took an item off of my life-stuff-to-figure-out list, but now that adds more questions as well.

I know who my birth parents are, but I'm no closer to knowing how the parents that raised me came to have me in their possession. We also don't know why they were hiding me or what they knew was coming.

Does it have to do with the prophecy stuff that India overheard? Could it really all be connected?

Andrei obviously accepts me, but what if they don't want me? What if I don't want to be a princess in another world?

"GODDAMMIT!"

That was supposed to be a frustrated scream in my head, but it came out of my mouth instead, and Andrei and Roman both jumped.

The other men took off just a bit ago to give us time to talk and think. Probably to give me time to get my shit together.

"I'm sorry."

"You have nothing to apologize for," Roman says gently as he pulls me back into his embrace. "Like everything else, we'll figure this out at whatever speed you need," he finishes with a kiss on my head.

"What's my name?"

They both turn to look at me.

"The princess. What was her...er, my name?" I ask more confidently.

"Larina," they answer in unison.

"But that doesn't matter. Your name doesn't matter to any of us. You matter," Roman quickly adds while Andrei nods in agreement.

"I don't want to upset you any further, but moth...I have a

letter from the King and Queen for if I ever found you. When you're ready, you can have it. Like everything else, as Roman said, we'll do this at your pace. No one wants to drag you to Zabella and disrupt your life any further. I'm just so glad I found you. And when you're ready, they will be too."

I nod. Another single tear skitters down my cheek, but I pull myself to my feet. "Thank you, Andrei." I hug my big brother. My twin. My single tear's friends join the party, and he pulls me closer with a sniffle of his own.

He pulls back, holding my shoulders an arm length away. "I'll leave you two to enjoy the rest of the evening. Just let me know if you need anything." And then he walks away, heading back to join the others around the fire.

I slowly turn to where Roman took my seat on the log. He smiles warmly at me with a look that says he's sorry and wishes he could take all this shit away for me. I plop myself onto his lap, wrapping my arms around his neck, and inhale his scent. I continue sitting here, taking all the calming his touch and smell provide, until I'm ready to move.

"I don't know why my life has turned out the way that it has, but it gave me you. Fuck, I really don't know what I'd do without you." I tuck myself into his body, wishing there was a way to live attached to him for the rest of my life. Nothing could get me if I was a literal part of his body.

But that's not how it works. My life and the universe continue to pelt me with information and things I never fathomed, and it only continues to make me stronger. This will too.

He holds me as long as I need it. Slowly rubbing circles on my back and thighs. Murmuring sweet words of comfort. Making me feel like somehow everything might actually be okay.

I pull away from his chest, wipe any tears or snot off my face from crying, take his face in my hands, and kiss him like the world is ending. Once he's registered his surprise, he answers my call and consumes me equally, allowing everything else to fade away for a few blissful moments.

When we come up for air, chests heaving, I smile. "Okay, Big Guy, how can I shift back into my wolf? I want more time with her."

The smile that overtakes his face should be chiseled into one of the statues in Italy. People would come from all over the world and other realms just to look at him. It's ridiculous how gorgeous he is, if I'm being honest.

"Just like you shifted back, that's all it takes to shift now that you've done it. Concentrate. Visualize yourself shifting into your wo—"

He doesn't finish because I've already shifted and am now bounding around him in circles. As a freaking wolf!

He smiles and turns to continue watching me go around him in circles a few more times before he reaches for me. He runs his hands through my fur, and a shiver runs through my body while my wolf purrs. He takes my furry face in his large hands, which now just look normal sized against my wolf, and kisses the end of my nose. "You're still the most breathtaking creature I've ever seen."

My wolf howls with happiness, many of the others joining in because Roman warned me it's contagious, like yawns are for people.

I jump back from him, leaning back and hopping around a bit, trying to convey that I want him to shift with me.

This will be so much easier when we can just communicate

telepathically.

He laughs at my antics but seems to understand because he peels his clothes from his body—*I think I just drooled. Like literally drooled because I'm a wolf*—then shifts.

I'd gotten used to our bond thrumming between us, waiting for us to complete it, but I did not expect the intensity of how it would feel as a wolf. With our wolves essentially being our souls, and the bond being tethered between souls, it literally feels like a giant magnet shoving us together. Like, when I'm not with him, I feel like I can't breathe.

I run to him, and, *Jesus,* I'm still tiny! He's still so much bigger than me.

His wolf walks around mine a few times before stopping just in front of me. His blue eye glowing darker, while his green eye glows brighter. *Do my eyes glow like that as a wolf?*

I approach him, tucking myself beneath his chin and nuzzle into his neck. He nuzzles me in return, then leans away and licks the top of my head.

His head whips to the right, just before Benny's wolf comes crashing into us, and I swear, I can feel his laughter all around me.

The twin's gray wolves are hot on his heels. I manage to dodge out of the way in time for them to start a dog pile on top of Roman. Slate's black wolf somehow portrays the same bored look he always has on his face. If I wasn't a wolf right now, I'd be giggling.

Andrei's brindled wolf approaches slowly, as if seeking permission. I make a dramatic show of trying to smile and wag my tail. I know my tail is moving, but I'm not sure what my wolf smile looks like on the outside; though, it seems to work because he slowly approaches and sits down right next to me. I allow myself to lean into him for a moment. Understanding our bond and wondering what could have been.

I shake the somber thoughts away, literally shaking my whole wolf's body.

Roman finally escapes the rowdy dog pile and makes a grumbly noise, tossing his head to the side, which I interpret as "Wanna go for a run?"

Instead of answering, I take off running. Roman and all the men following. I think Andrei howls, and the sound fills me up until I too have to howl, or I might explode.

The howl is filled with happiness and hope. And in this moment, as I run through the forest with my mate, my twin, and our family, I feel so powerful and free. It feels like I'm flying. The wind in my face tastes like possibility.

And maybe, just maybe, it will all be okay after all.

44
ROMAN

I don't know why I continue to be surprised by her strength. No matter what information she gets hit with, it only knocks her down long enough for her to properly gather it and store it the way she needs to until she's ready to address it herself.

She just got told she has a twin brother, royal parents, and that she's the lost princess of Zabella, and after a couple minutes of snuggles, she had completely compartmentalized the entire ordeal.

Now we're running through the forest, and I can't take my eyes off of her. I wouldn't if I could. The way her wolf's silver fur glistens in the moonlight is mesmerizing. The way she flies between the trees, you can't even tell her feet touch the ground. If this were one of her Disney movies, there would be a trail of sparkles billowing behind her.

But this isn't a movie. This is really happening.

My mate is the lost princess.

Potentially kidnapped by my father not once, but twice now.

And what is he after?

I'm trying to take Leera's lead and tuck those thoughts and feelings away until it's time to sit down and unpack everything, but, fuck, it's hard. How does she do this? It's nearly all she's done since she came crashing into my life.

I've always attacked my problems as they presented themselves, sometimes literally. I thought it was a productive process until I met her. She continues to do nothing less than provide a better way to live. A better way to be. I haven't realized it before, but maybe going through everything that we've both been through is exactly what made us perfect for each other.

When we finally make it back to the pack, the men branch off to their own cabins, while I lead Leera to mine. It's tucked further into the woods on a hill overlooking the rest of the pack. The view of the pack with the lake behind it and the wall of trees in the background is something I've taken for granted. I don't spend enough time here, and now I wonder if I ever really will. With her being the princess, our lives could change a whole lot more than I thought.

As we approach the cabin's front porch, I shift and turn to Leera. When she shifts, she stumbles into me, and everywhere our bodies touch feels like a lightning storm on a humid summer night.

Since we've just shifted, we're already missing our clothes, which Leera just seems to have noticed, if I had to judge by the blush on her cheeks.

In an effort to chase her insecurities away, I trail my fingers over her lush curves, all the way up her body, until my hands rest on the back of her head. I rub my thumbs just behind her ears and watch goosebumps trail down her arms.

"I think I might be ready," she whispers and stares up at me.

"I want you to know you're ready, my little miracle. Furthermore, I don't want to take you for the first time around a bunch of nosey wolves and your brother. I want your first time to be as special as you are, Princess."

She's blushing furiously, but she nods. "That makes sense. Does that mean we can't do *anything?*" she asks with her bottom lip between her teeth.

Tsking, I say, "Now, I didn't say that. I still have to reward you for your first shift. You've been such a good girl." I purr, and she melts into me. I take advantage of the moment and lift her against me, wrapping her legs around my body as I hold her by the smooth cheeks of her ass.

"H-how will you reward me?"

Walking into the cabin, I take the stairs to the loft two at a time. I kiss my way across her jawline to her ear, nibbling on her earlobe when we reach the bed. "Why don't we see how many times you can come before the sun rises?" I breathe.

She shudders beneath me. "Wh-what about you?"

"I fear I won't be able to control myself because of the full moon, and we can't have that, my lady."

I trail my fingers up her stomach to the perfect mounds of her breasts, heaving with every breath. "Is that alright with you? Tell me what you want."

She nods, arching into my touch.

"Tell me. Should I touch you here?" I roll her peaked nipple between my thumb and forefinger.

"Ahh, yes," she moans.

"What about here?" I lazily drift my other finger to her core, barely grazing her wet clit.

"God, yes, please, Roman," she pants.

"As you wish, Your Majesty," I growl, and her eyes narrow for a moment before she realizes I'm moving to kneel between her legs.

I spread her legs further apart so I can see all of her glistening and ready for me, the scent of her arousal filling my lungs. She begins to wriggle and arch, searching for friction while I am lost in a trance. With the spell broken, I lean in, licking the full length of her lips, and suckle her bundle of nerves into my mouth gently.

"Oh...my...Roman, please."

Which I decide means, *Please, add your finger to my sweet pink pussy.*

As I slide it in, I continue to work her clit with my tongue. I slide in slowly, as she's still growing accustomed to the feel of it.

"More, more, more," she begs.

I pull my mouth away from her, remove my finger, causing her to cry out, and lift her head to investigate what's going on. That's the moment I choose to slide my finger into my mouth to lick her nectar off of my skin. After consuming every last drop, she's a writhing mess of need. I remove my finger from my mouth and replace it with both that finger and my middle finger.

Maintaining eye contact with her, I take my two wet fingers and slowly glide them into her hot core. She throws her head back and moans my name. When I reach the point of resistance, I stop and allow her to lead, telling me when she's ready to continue. "Deep breaths, baby, you're doing so good."

"I'm ready, keep going. Please, keep going."

I lean back into her, lapping at her clit while playing her body like an instrument until she screams, coming apart on my tongue. I work her through until the spasms fade and crawl up next to her so that I can see her face.

"That was one," she says with her eyes closed before pulling herself up onto her elbows and giving me a devilish grin. "But I won't accept any more until I get to play. You said I was a good girl, wasn't I?" she pouts, and how can I say no to that?

45
Leera

The answer is seven.

In case you were wondering how many times we took turns providing each other with orgasms until I'm pretty sure I literally passed out from the last one and slept until morning.

I feel like I'm glowing. I definitely haven't stopped smiling. He said he didn't want to take me here because of the nosey werewolves, but there is no way they didn't hear my screams and his roars last night.

I expected to be a little embarrassed this morning, but everyone is acting like they couldn't hear us all night. Maybe they couldn't. Or maybe it's because they're all werewolves, some having found their mate. Maybe sex isn't such a taboo topic in some realms.

Like the one I'm a freaking princess of. I'm still working on wrapping my head around all of that, but it makes more sense than anything else so far. Like why I was homeschooled, and we traveled all the time. Why I was given wolfsbane my whole life. Possibly why my parents were taken from me. Why I was kidnapped. It's all still a load of shit for anyone to go through, but the more we learn, the more the puzzle starts to look like a picture instead of a blotchy mess within a flimsy frame.

We're packing up the little bit of luggage we brought with us. "When can we come back? I love it here," I ask Roman.

"Unfortunately, the season just started, so we can't come out here for a day or night for a while. Plus, there's your school work, and the internet out here isn't reliable since we have no cell service. But outside of those things, we can come here whenever you like." He smiles.

"Until I'm the found princess and my whole life changes," I say, kicking a rock on our way to the car.

He sets his stuff on the ground, stops in front of me, takes my chin in his hands, and brings my eyes to his. "Your life will not change any more than you want it to. I don't care if they're the king and queen, you are my mate, and I swear, I will not let them make you do anything. Understand?"

I nod my head because once again, words fail me when he gets all intense like this for me. It also makes me a little wet in the britches if you catch my drift.

I told him I thought I was ready last night, but after last night, I know I'm ready. In case he doesn't have as much control as he thinks, I want to make sure I have the one solid thing in my life—him. I know mates are taken seriously, but I don't want to leave any room for any potential discussions, separation, or the like.

I'm also really tired of them sharing their silent conversations without me. I want to be able to reach him at all times.

Most of all, I'm just really ready to be his. Completely.

We had lunch with the pack and said our goodbyes to Jeanine and Meredith. Miss Tilly got teary-eyed as we left without her sister, but they each promised to take turns visiting more. Roman told her she could stay as long as she wanted, but she wanted to come home with us.

Andrei loads into the car with us, claiming to be tired from last night, but I have a feeling it's just so we can spend more time together. If he'd just ask, I'd tell him anything he wants to know that he hasn't already gotten from me being with Roman.

The twins, Benny, and Slate are running beside the car as we drive down the small street to the end of the forest. The sun is shining, and the new day feels less heavy than everything did last night. I'm staring at the obnoxiously-handsome side of Roman's head when all of our phone alerts start going off at once with a number of missed calls and voicemail messages.

They're all from Khaos, and there's even a few from India. My hands are shaking so badly while we wait for him to answer Roman's call. We've stopped the car and rolled the windows down so the other men know what's going on as well.

"Pick up. Pick up. Pick up," I whisper-chant to myself.

He doesn't answer. Roman ends the call and immediately redials his number, laying his hand on my thigh and rubbing his thumb back and forth to comfort me.

He finally answers, but he sounds like hell, "Roman...we... were"—he coughs into the phone—"we...were...attacked."

Oh my god.

Our voices mesh together as we try to talk to him at the same time, Roman asking, "What do you mean attacked? By whom?" and me asking, "Where are you?" but the line goes dead.

I cling to the window of the car and cry, "Slate, help! Where's your laptop? Do you have service? Can you find him?"

Slate darts behind the car to shift, thankfully aware of my still not being used to naked men everywhere, because I was so upset I wouldn't have remembered to turn my head.

"I'm on it," he grunts as he rummages through the trunk for his stuff.

"Andrei, hop out, let Slate in, in case he doesn't quite have service so I can drive farther to where he needs to be," Roman commands. Though he doesn't even have to finish because Andrei immediately understands what he needs, and he swings his door open and steps out.

Slate gets in the car, and Andrei offers me a nod before closing the door.

I'm trying to keep my shit together and not cry AGAIN when Slate finally makes his sound that means "ah-ha, I got it."

"What, where are they?"

"He's right on the edge of the forest of his pack lands," he says while turning his laptop around to show us.

"That's so far away," I cry, because I have no idea what to do.

"Eris, Dolos, Andrei, go back to the pack and gather Jeanine and a couple others to help. And supplies. Tell them we're taking a plane, and we're flying out in an hour," Roman says with a stern nod that they return.

"Oh my goodness," Miss Tilly says to herself.

I grab my phone and dial India's number again, but I've called her five times now, and she's still not answering.

"Slate, check Khaos and India's locations. Are they still together?"

After a few moments of furious typing, he nods.

"What can I do? I need to do something!" I beg.

Roman turns to me, taking both my hands in his and says, "Leera, focus. It's going to be okay. You keep trying to call them. Can you do that for me?"

I nod.

"Slate, get that plane ready."

"Already on it, Boss."

46
ROMAN

We're in the air, and I'm trying to prepare Leera for what she might see, but I don't think she's truly understanding the severity of a situation like this. If Khaos was so injured that he sounded like that and had to call us for help, that means that something very bad has happened.

Khaos, while not one of my favorite people in the worlds, is almost as strong as I am. Coupled with our werewolf healing, and for him to be in that kind of shape means it's far worse than she understands.

Scenario after scenario of what could have happened plays out in my mind over and over again during the nearly two-hour flight to where his pack resides in Maine.

I'm also balancing trying to keep Leera calm while planning strategy with the men in the event that the assailants are still nearby. Though I doubt anyone would expect that Khaos would reach out to me, especially if it's my father that is involved.

I'm so fucking proud of my mate. She hasn't had a panic attack, and she's keeping her anxiety in control even with everything that's been thrown at her the last twenty-four hours. I don't know if finally uniting with her wolf has given her the additional strength or if it's just who she is.

Up to this point, I've been able to be the doting, hockey playing, lovesick pup for her, and I worry what she'll think when she has to see the other side of me. The commander of a royal military. The warrior who does what's needed, no matter the cost. The mate who will burn down the realms for her.

What if that side of me is too much for her?
What if she's too light for my darkness?
What if my darkness kills her like my father's killed my mother?

I shake the negative thoughts plaguing me, knowing that if there is a being in this universe that can handle me, it's the little spitfire sitting next to me, staring out the window. The Goddess gave her to me for a reason. I will not let either of them down.

The fasten seat belts sign blinks to life, indicating that we're going to begin our descent.

"Hey, Princess. Are you okay?" I ask, pulling her belt around her and clicking it in place.

She smiles, but it's weak and worried. "I just hope he's okay. We just got to start getting to know each other. And if he's hurt this badly, what about India? If they're at his pack, is his pack okay? Is this all because of me again? Have more people been hurt because of me?"

"Shhhh," I soothe as I wipe a single tear off of her face. "No matter what we find, none of this is your fault. The only ones at fault are the people doing this. I promise you, no matter what we have to do or however long it takes, we will figure it all out and end this."

She nods and takes a deep breath, then asks, "Slate, were you able to find anything else?"

He meets her eyes and slowly shakes his head. "I'm sorry."

"We'll know what's going on soon enough. We're landing now," Benny says with a crooked, hopeful smile.

When we finally pull the car to a stop, just outside Khaos' territory, she flies out of the car without giving any of us a chance to make sure it's safe.

Move fast. Check the perimeter for any lingering threats, I instruct my men.

"Leera, where are you going?!" I shout as I sprint to catch up to her.

"To get my brother!" she yells back over her shoulder.

Their bond. She's following it. I realize.

Jeanine, you and the others follow us.

Thankful that my legs are longer than hers, it only takes me a minute to catch up to her. It felt like it took longer, knowing that she could be running head first into an attacker. All of a sudden, she jerks herself right, runs up two more steps, then stops in her tracks and screams.

47
Leera

The scream that escapes me without my consent hurts my throat nearly as much as my body and soul ache as I take in the scene in front of me.

There is quite literally a trail of dead bodies leading to Khaos. I try to talk to him, but there's blood everywhere, and the squelch of every step I take makes me gag.

Noticing my trouble, Roman picks me up and carries me to Khaos. I would say he's unphased by the blood, but that's the wrong word. He's definitely phased, just not in the same way as I am. Where I'm horrified and trying not to hurl my guts up, he's furious. The anger is radiating off of him in nearly visible waves.

I have to remind myself that he's seven hundred and thirteen years old and the commander of a werewolf army. Of course, he's unphased by the gore surrounding us.

When we finally reach where Khaos lies, I scramble out of his arms. He's hesitant to release me, but he finally gives in.

It takes all of my self-control not to launch myself at his tattered body to hold him close. I hover my hands around his body, begging it to hold on. If he looks like this hours after calling us, how bad did he look before? I know they have faster healing than people.

"Khaos," I choke. "Can you hear me?"

His eyes immediately flutter before he raises his eyelids about half way. "You came."

"What? Of course, we came. We're here," I cry, looking around at the devastation everywhere. "What happened?"

"Leera, honey, slow down. He needs Jeanine," Roman says softly.

"You'll be okay. You have to be okay." I continue to cry as I hold Khaos' hand against my chest when I hear a shaky intake of breath.

I lift my eyes to find Roman staring at me, his eyes wide in shock.

"Wh-what is it?" I whisper in case there's an attacker behind me.

He points at Khaos. "His arm," is all he says.

I look down, also gasping and jumping away from Khaos. "What's happening to him?!" I cry even harder, clasping my hands against my face, trying to hold in the pain.

There's a silver light barely glowing from his hand, slowly creeping up his arm to his shoulder.

The light continues across his shoulder, growing larger to cover his head and his chest. Spreading to his other arm and down the remainder of his body.

"This isn't possible." Everywhere the light travels, it…"This isn't possible," I say again, shaking my head.

Everywhere the light travels across his body, it leaves healthy, unmarred skin in its path.

Khaos is now able to open his eyes as the light from his head has gone out, and he's watching it consume his legs.

All of us stand in shock and awe at what's happening.

When the light goes out, no one says anything for a moment. We just stare at Khaos and glance at each other. The others are beginning to arrive behind us, and I still can't move.

"R-roman, what was that?"

But he's still stunned when Khaos responds, "Leera. It was... do you truly not know?"

"Me? Know what? What MORE don't I know?" I scream-sob.

"It was you. I don't know how or why, but you just...you just healed me," Khaos says with far too much seriousness, though still shocked himself.

I can't help but outright laugh at him. "I'm sorry, but that's just not possible. I'm a wolf. I met her. My par... the people who raised me were witches. Not me." I shake my head and cross my arms around myself.

Roman finally finds his voice. "Last night was your first shift," is all he says, mostly to himself. He lifts his eyes to mine. "Your shift. Sometimes, when a wolf shifts for the first time, they unlock something within themselves. Little things like having premonition-like feelings, being able to feel other wolves' energies, an even more heightened sense of smell, but I've never seen anything like this. You healed him. You can smell your scent all over him from your gift."

If the real world were like the cartoons, where jaws can fall until they literally hit the ground, that would be me right now.

I want to deny it. This is crazy. But as I go to say something, my wolf snorts at me like I've offended her.

This was you...er us?

She huffs in response.

I stare at my hands in disbelief. "It was me, us. My wolf...she confirmed it." I turn to look at Roman. "How?"

He shakes his head as his eyes change from shock to beaming with pride. "I don't know. The Goddess does everything with a reason."

Khaos rises from the ground to stand beside us, just as the others approach. His clothes and hair are still covered in blood, and Lord knows what else, but he's whole. He wraps his arms around me and whispers in my ear, "You saved me," and squeezes me one more time before pulling away.

Everyone stands in shock for a moment, just staring at us.

"Later," Roman says firmly. "We have plenty here that still need our attention."

When the realization hits me, I shout, "Wait, where's India?"

Khaos spins on his heel and lurches over about ten feet, where a mangled body is leaned against a tree. "India, they're here," is all he says as he shakes and tries to wake her.

Having completed my first shift, my hearing is now exponentially better than it was before, and when I lean towards her, I can barely hear her heart beating, and she's struggling to breathe. I frantically turn to Khaos and say, "I don't know how I healed you. What do I do?"

Roman leans down with us and scoops a tear from my cheek that had just fallen. "Your tears are shimmering. They weren't doing this in the car or on the plane, but there wasn't anyone injured. It's the only thing that comes close to making sense right now."

He wipes the tear on India's forehead, and the light shimmers but flickers instead of consuming her like it did for Khaos.

"Lee-ra," she breathes raggedly.

"Shh, I'm trying to help—"

She grabs my arm, shaking her head. "It's...too...late..." She tries to take a large rattling breath, but it makes her cough and blood drips from her lips. "I...wa-wanted...to say...I'm so...ry..." She coughs again.

My tears continue to shimmer and fall, but when I wipe them on her, they only flicker for a moment. I wipe a few on her chest, hoping to at least ease her pain.

"I forgive you," I cry, because even though we absolutely hate each other, no one deserves this. She was trying to help. I've never seen someone die. The light on her chest flickers a little more than the others but still sputters out after only a few seconds.

"Be a...g-good...q-queen. Save the...r-realms. D-don't...let...th-them...win..."

"I don't know how to do that." I look around at the men who have all kneeled around us, Jeanine standing behind me crying with the couple of women that came with her to help. "I don't know how to do any of this. But I promise, they won't win anything. I promise."

She closes her eyes and nods before her body stills, and I swear, I can feel her soul wrap around my body before lifting to the sky.

In unison, we all howl for the soul lost. She may not have been a good person, but she was still a wolf. A person. She may have deserved to get her ass kicked, but no one deserves to be mutilated and murdered for power.

When we've finished howling, my ears perk to the left as I

hear another howl, much further away.

"That's n-not possible," Khaos says before he takes off running so fast that I can only gape at him.

Roman scoops me up and begins running after Khaos. Benny, Andrei, and Slate are on our heels.

"The whole pack was slaughtered. Whoever attacked them, they killed everyone, and they didn't leave a single scent to trace," Benny informs us.

The weight of his words hits me square in the chest. "They killed an entire pack?"

"They were likely hunting India and killed them because Khaos was helping her," Andrei says from behind me.

We slow as Khaos weaves through his decimated pack lands. The homes are still smoldering with embers when we approach.

I throw myself out of Roman's arms, and a feral scream rips from my lungs as I take in the devastation in front of me. There are still traces of anguish and terror drifting through what's left of the trees. In a rage, I whip around to face them.

Roman, my mate, my love, my safe place.

Andrei, my twin brother, my other kind of other half.

Benny, the sunshine that kept Roman together in my absence.

Slate, the serious tech wizard who tries not to care.

Eris and Dolos, the twins, wild most of the time but serious when it counts.

"We have to stop them! Tell me what to do! They did this because of me!" I scream and fall to the ground.

Roman crashes to the earth beside me and pulls me onto his lap. I can feel him nod, but he can feel the devastation coursing through my body. I can feel the pain and the hate here. It's still radiating all around me.

"I mean it, Roman. I've never done anything like this in my life, but we have to do something!"

I'm still yelling, and I can't stop the pain in my chest over all the souls lost over this. Over me.

"I don't care what we have to do. I don't care if I have to throw my life away to become a fucking princess if that means I have an army of werewolves at my disposal to take care of this."

Roman squeezes me tighter. "We'll take care of it—"

"Together," I say firmly. I'm not budging on this.

"Together," all six men promise as one.

"No one fucks with my pucking family. Not my family. Not my people. Not my friends. Not my enemies. This is wrong."

48
ROMAN

Leera's declaration is immediately followed by Khaos shouting, "Over here!"

She turns to me with wide eyes and takes off running towards his voice. She stumbles over a rock and cries out when she realizes it's not a rock but a skull, belonging to someone from his pack.

I pull her to me, trying to shield her from the death and anguish surrounding us. I lift her, carrying her the rest of the way to where he's standing behind a home, where a tree has fallen over a cellar door.

I set her down gently. My men and I walk over and each take a place at the tree. My heart is pounding in my chest, and my wolf is restless. I look over to Leera to make sure she's safe. She's just staring at me with wide and hopeful eyes.

I shake the weird feeling off and focus on lifting this massive tree away from the door. The men gather round, and we all lift when Benny calls, "Now."

Once we've cleared the door, Khaos pulls it open. Leera begins to lean in to help, but I snatch her back. We don't know who or what is down there, and she's definitely not going to be the one to find out.

Khaos steps into the cellar, and a few minutes later, he comes out with a woman I've never seen before, but my wolf takes notice. That's when I notice she looks oddly familiar. She's got long, dark hair, so dark it's almost black, but you can tell in the sun that it's still brown. She also has the brightest green eyes I've seen in a very long time…nearly seven hundred years.

"It's not possible," I breathe, while the bond thumps between us.

Leera's attention swings to me with worry, and she jolts towards me. "Roman, what's wrong?"

"Speak!" I demand of the stranger.

"I'm sorry, Roman, you weren't supposed to know," she says meekly, with all eyes on her.

"Who the fuck are you?" I roar.

She doesn't even flinch.

"What are you talking about? She's been a part of my pack since nearly the beginning," Khaos joins the conversation.

"It was the only place I didn't think I'd ever run into you," she tells me.

Leera's growing irritated now. "Look, we have enough going on here without you hovering around whatever has him all riled up," she finishes, wiggling her fingers between us to emphasize her point.

She smiles at Leera weakly before she turns to me. "You're not supposed to know I exist. You're not supposed to know what he did to her…" she trails off and hangs her head.

"WHO. ARE. YOU?!" I command with my alpha energy.

She's visibly trying to hold it in until she can't any longer, "I'm sorry, Roman. I'm your sister."

to be continued.

Acknowledgements

insert squealing

I just finished the second round of self-edits on My Pucking Family as I write this, and oh my gosh, I love this story and my characters so much!

I hope you love them even a fraction as much as I do.

I hope this book answered a lot of your questions but also raised some new ones that we'll have to investigate together.

I know as a reader, I've always hated cliffhangers, so I first want to offer a sincere, from-the-heart apology for the continued cliffies, but they really just give the story a certain level of thrill that I now understand as an author and hereby vow to never complain about again. Hush Di, I can feel you snickering from here.

Speaking of Di, thank you again for…fuck…just for everything. Not only do I believe in soul mates and know I found that in my husband, but I also believe that sometimes you have a soul mate that isn't romantic. I believe with all my heart that you are my soul sister, and I can't imagine my life without you. I love you.

Speaking of my husband, Happy Birthday, baby. Since I released My Pucking Mate on my birthday, I asked if we could take over his birthday to celebrate the second book, and he graciously let us steal his birthday. You know how much I love you.

To my Omega—my fucking epic street team—I would be so fucking lost without all of you. Dammit, I'm crying again; shut up, Mari. The continued love that you all share for me, my books, my characters…there aren't appropriate words in the English dictionary to ever convey what you all mean to me. I wouldn't have gotten this far without you. NONE of this would be possible without you. To Mari's morning voice messages that bring me light on the darkest days. To Erin for the cutest stickers that you take the extra time to add. To Coco for the leopard print that fills my cup. To Liz for being as obsessed with my characters and Pooh Bear as me. To Madison for the raging pink love for my book that makes me smile when I need it the most. Gosh, there are so many of you that bring different levels of happiness, love, and light to my life: Nikki, Alyssa, Jenny, Faith, Nancy, Brandi, Crystal, Ashley, Tiffany, Jade, Sage, Audrey, Danielle, Sam, Kaija, Angie, April, Ash, Ashlee, Bec, Bianca, Brandy, Danes, Kay, Kaycee, Liz, Mars, Whitney…gosh, just all of you! If I didn't list you, I swear, it doesn't mean I don't love you; that would just be a lot of names!

To my editor & hypewoman, Jaquelyn, thank you for helping me make my books become the best they can be!!

To my formatter, Aurelia, you literally haven't even touched this book yet, and I know I'm going to adore everything you do because that's who you are.

To Bedpost Books for having me at your store and making my indie author dreams come true: make friends with the sweetest little bookstore owner.

Thank you again to all my author besties—D. Raven, C.R. Jane, Stacy Williams, and K. Iwancio—that let me continue to ask you a barrage of questions. Thank you for being the supportive and amazing women you are!

As always, the most important thank you goes to YOU. The reader who's continuously supporting not only me but everyone out there with a dream. You're the real MVP, and none of this could happen without you.

Last, most certainly not least—my absolutely amazing, more-than-slightly-feral Street Team—specifically those of you that were crazy enough to band together to raise money for the spicy art of Roman and Leera, but also a printer so I can make us all the amazing things. I constantly say that I couldn't do this without yall but you REALLY don't understand how much you mean to me. Yall are the heart and soul of why my books are being seen by the literal world. There aren't accurate words to truly portray what you all mean to me. The NSFW Art was comissioned by: Samantha Mackey, Mari, Dayna, Alyssa, Danielle Pettyjohn, Holly Clover, Amy Key, Brandi Augustine, Cori, Micca Burris, Coco, Kat Eckerson, Erin, Leslie King, Tanisha Woods, Brandy McCoy, Courtney R, Sarah Parks, Tash Sainsbury, @faithlynsey_reads, Mars, Lindsay Adams, Michaella Mosier, Angela Stephens, Lisa Haines, Ashlee Settle, Natalie @good.fkn.girl, Crystal @spicysundaymorning, Bianca Valiente, @kristynlovesbooks, Morgan, Jen @twisted.page, Amber Tentnowski, @yerawizardsaraaa, Whitley, @books.withgenna, Ashley Hodges, Chantel, Angel, Destiny, Althea Ball, Nikki, Erin Schenk-Hardee.

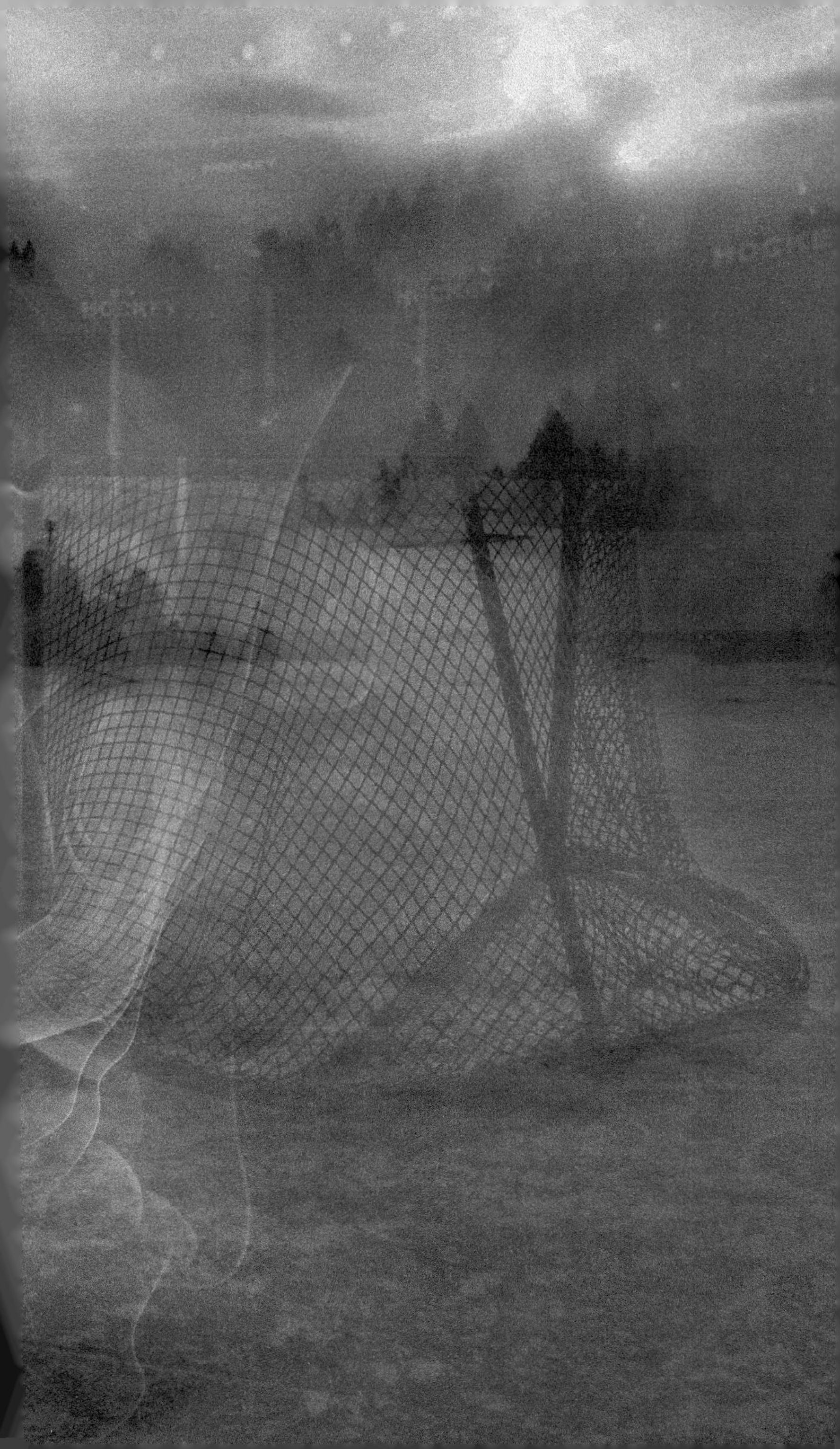

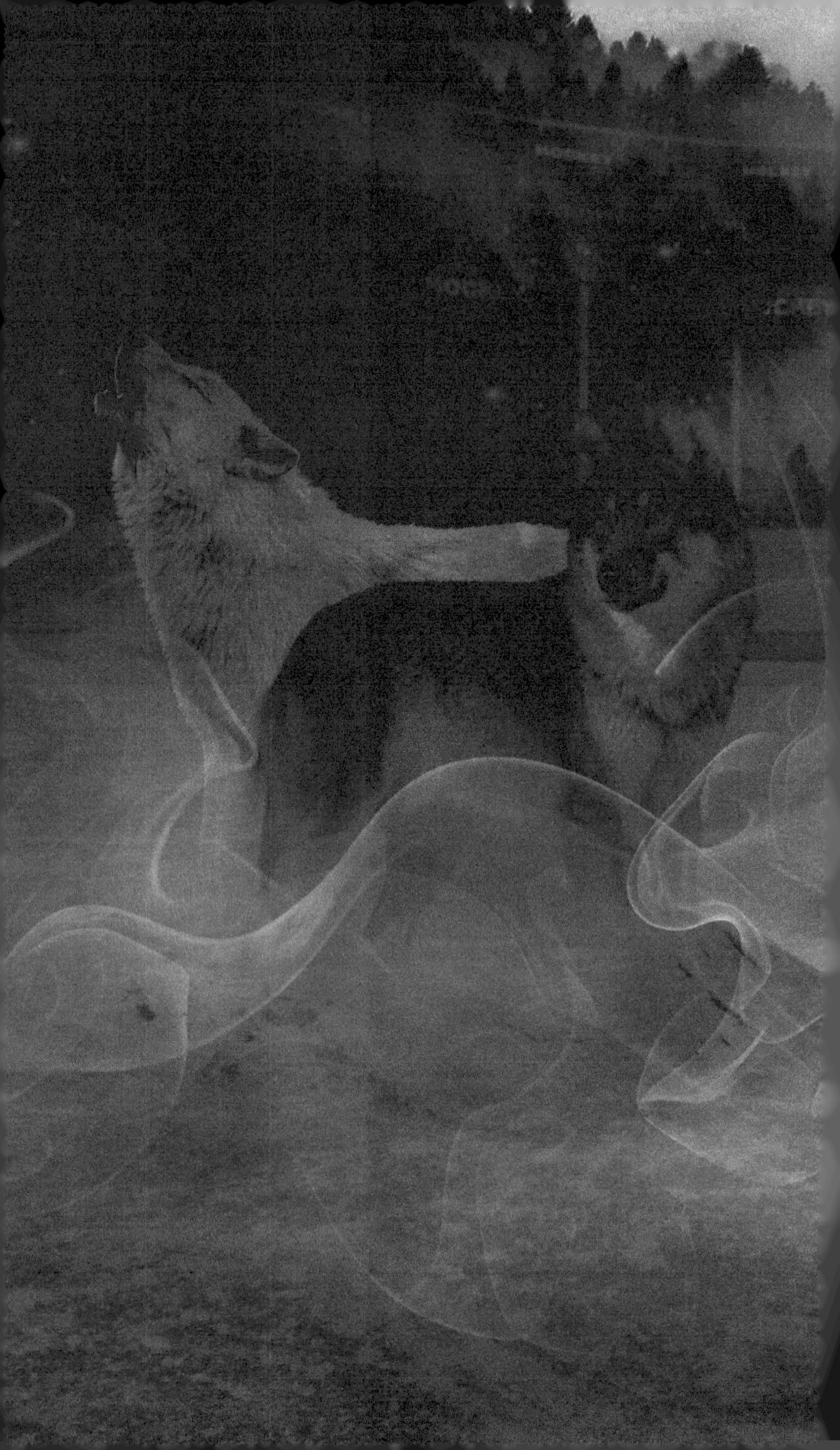

About the Author

Hey y'all, Izzy here!
Still a Midwest mom of four.
Still working full time in the real world.
Still reading, writing, traveling, walking, & shopping.
Still on Instagram & TikTok under IzzyElliottWrites and also now with a new website: izzyelliott.com for signed books, book boxes, merch, and more!